Jean E Foster

4th Set Nov 1993

Forever 🌹 *Romances*

Windsong

Elee Landress

Forever ❧ Romances

is an imprint of
Guideposts Associates, Inc.
Carmel, NY 10512

To my husband
Jim

This Guideposts edition is published by special arrangement
with Thomas Nelson Communications.

Printed in the United States of America.

Scripture quotations in this book are from the King James Version
of the Bible.

ISBN 0-8407-7359-5

Chapter One

Ashley stood beside her gray Escort. She inhaled the heady scent of orange blossoms and gazed at the deserted, pink-stucco mansion with frank curiosity. As a student majoring in design, she had often wondered what her first assignment would be when she became a fully licensed interior decorator. Never in her wildest imagination had she dreamed her fledgling career would begin deep in the grovelands of Florida's largest citrus empire!

Her deep blue eyes were bright with interest as she studied the classic Spanish architecture of the mansion. She was excited at the rare opportunity it afforded her, for few such estates had survived the twentieth century. Most decorators only dreamed about this kind of project—and now it was her very first commission.

Unconsciously tucking a strand of lustrous blonde hair behind her ear, she assessed the mansion. Sagging shutters dangled from high arched windows, their leaded panes staring across an overgrown lawn. Missing red tiles left toothless black spaces in the roof, giving the house a forlorn appearance. Still the place had a charm unspoiled by time and neglect. Just beyond, a crystal lake lapped rhythmically on the white sand. It was the only sound in the sultry April morning.

Could it really be the first day of April already, she

thought in surprise. So much had happened since she left unemployment and the snowy streets of Chicago to seek refuge at her late grandfather's winter cottage in Florida. It seemed a year had passed instead of a mere two months. She pulled her wandering thoughts back and looked nervously around her. The silence was disquieting, and she was suddenly aware of her isolation.

Orange trees stood in military formation, marching as far as the eye could see until they became green dots on the horizon. Australian pines stood like sentinels around the grove, a living wall against storm winds that would otherwise destroy the harvest. Shading her eyes, she searched the road through the grove for some sign of a vehicle. Her client was late.

Ashley picked her way across the broken concrete sidewalk leading to the palm court entrance of the mansion. She carefully skirted the tangled masses of flame vine and wild yellow roses which had overgrown the walkway, pushed aside a draping arch of purple bougainvillea that clutched at her fall of honey-colored hair. Something skittered in the knee-high grass, and Ashley hurried forward to the marble-paved palm court. There she paused in awe of the color around her. Flared hibiscus bloomed in pink profusion. Urns cascaded with purple phlox gone wild. Yellow tree roses and ferns surrounded the dry marble fountains—and with only a little imagination Ashley could visualize their cool droplets sparkling in the sun.

Reaching the shady veranda, she perched on its balustrade, smoothed the skirt of her white linen suit, and drew a note pad from her leather briefcase. As she waited her curiosity about Marcos Perone mounted.

The Perone family had been one of the first to settle in Avon Park and had given the small community its citrus industry—a part of their Spanish heritage. She scanned notes she had made at the local library. One of the first Perones had politically paved the way for the railroad from Jacksonville to Miami which had meant so much to Florida's industrial development. Another Perone had aided the Seminole tribe by negotiating a peace treaty on the banks of a river still known as Peace River. This, and more, she had gleaned from the helpful librarian, but no information was on file about the current generation of Perones.

Casual inquiries among the local residents revealed that Marcos Perone, her client, had operated his own oil fields in Alaska for the last ten years. He had returned home to take over Perone Citrus Enterprises when a tragic yachting accident killed his parents and his only brother and his sister-in-law. Their children, a boy and girl, had fortunately not been with the yachting party, and they now lived with Marcos. Beyond that, no one seemed to know much about his current interests and social habits, things Ashley found helpful to know about a potential client. Apparently, Marcos Perone lived in seclusion.

Pacing restlessly to the ornate, double-front doors, she peered through the windows. Suddenly they were thrust open and Ashley fell backward, startled by glittering black eyes that stared at her from beneath high arched brows. She gaped at the sophisticated woman before her, the sleek cap of black hair, the red slash of a mouth. She appeared to be in her mid-thirties. Quickly regaining her composure, Ashley extended her hand.

"Hello," she smiled. "I'm Ashley Ames of Signature Interiors."

The hand that shook hers was noticeably hard. Oversized rings cut into Ashley's palm. "My name is Sydney Ogleby," the woman replied, without warmth or welcome. "I presume you expected Mr. Perone?"

Ashley nodded. "We had a ten o'clock appointment. I didn't see a car and thought no one was here."

"My Mercedes is parked in the side portico. Mr. Perone is absorbed with business and will not be joining us. He has delegated this little project to me."

Ashley followed her into the wide foyer and mounted

7

marble steps to a large living area of ballroom proportions. Its walls vaulted two stories to the ceiling and a balcony surrounded the main floor on all four sides. *Little was hardly the word to describe it,* thought Ashley. Massive arched windows of etched glass provided a lake view. A stuccoed fireplace spanned one end of the room, and on the other a stairway spiraled to the second floor. Never in her life had she seen anything as wonderful! In sheer exhilaration she wheeled and faced her guide.

"How fortunate you are to have an employer who trusts you to restore his home!"

Sydney bristled. "Mr. Perone is not my employer, he is my fiance!" she snapped. Immediately she bit her lip and frowned. "We have not made a public announcement, so naturally I expect you to treat this as professional privileged information," she said haughtily.

"Of course," Ashley agreed, annoyed with Sydney's condescending attitude. She reminded Ashley of a model in a magazine cigarette ad. Her red dress was overpoweringly dramatic, and enormous gold loop earrings quivered with the slightest movement of her sleekly coiffed head.

Quietly, Ashley inquired, "You will be making the decisions about the house, then?"

"Yes, I can't imagine why Marc wants to keep this old relic. It's going to be devilishly difficult to transform it into a contemporary style."

Ashley listened in dismay as Sydney described the look she wanted—a twenty-first-century Hollywood movie set completely at odds with the classical architecture of the mansion.

When she had concluded, Ashley suggested as tactfully as possible that when working with a very pronounced style, it was better to conform to that style than to try to change it radically. She pointed out the virtues of the existing architecture—the high, arched, leaded windows that were the work of an artist, and the hand-painted tiles on the floor that were irreplaceable. Meissen vases flanked the mantle, and hand-hammered iron grilles bannistered the balcony.

"A cosmetic face lift might be all that's needed to make this room very pleasing."

Sydney looked at her aghast. "Heavens! Surely you're not suggesting that we leave the place as it is? I have no intention of living in a museum!" She waved a brace-leted arm toward the wall of arched windows. "I want those replaced with fixed glass panels, and I've already ordered wall-to-wall carpet for the entire house!"

Oblivious to Ashley's grim silence, Sydney moved on to the oval dining room walled in pale green silk im-ported from China. She instructed Ashley to get a cost estimate for remodeling the room into a conventional rectangular shape.

Ashley noted the gilt-framed oil portraits of the Perone men and the busts of women resting in wall niches. "What do you want to do with those?" she asked, entranced by their loveliness.

"Who cares? Make a bonfire of them if you want!"

In the kitchen, Sydney disclaimed any interest, saying she would employ a full-time housekeeper-cook. The antiquated plumbing would have to be replaced, and the wall behind the wood stove torn out in the process. It looked as though an old fireplace was hidden behind the wall. The kitchen's only redeeming features were its large size and ample windows.

Sydney led the way to the library. "This is the only room now occupied. It has a private entrance from the front veranda, so Marc uses it for private conferences he does not wish to conduct in his downtown office. It is off-limits, but you can look around for a moment if you like."

The room was furnished with a hand-carved mahog-any desk that Ashley suspected was an original from Spain. The library table was flanked with high-backed leather chairs and, of course, walls of leather-bound volumes. An antique wall clock ticked away the minutes from lifetime to lifetime.

As they left the library and crossed the ballroom toward the stairway, Ashley saw guest quarters down a hallway leading to the side portico. Mounting the stairs, she admired the carving of fruit and blossoms on the handrail. There was no time to examine the wood, but she suspected it was an exotic import.

They crossed the balcony to the children's wing and entered a sunlit room with window seats under bay windows. A maple rocker stood in one corner, well-used and battle-scarred. Toy shelves stood against another wall and were still lined with their boyish collections. In the middle of the room stood a rocking horse with a tattered rope mane.

"This was Marc's room when he was a boy," said Sydney. She flipped through a dusty volume of *Robinson Crusoe* and wrinkled her nose. "All of this stuff ought to be junked."

Ashley marveled at her coldness. To most women the boyhood memorabilia of a fiance would have been treasures; to Sydney it was trash.

An adjoining bath led to an identical bedroom which had belonged to Marc's younger brother, the one who had died so tragically.

"Are these the rooms the niece and nephew will have?"

Sydney nodded, expressionless.

A soft light came into Ashley's eyes. It would be fun to do these rooms. "What are the children like? How old are they?"

"Oh, they're like all kids. I have a responsible position with the bank, you know, and I don't have the time to get involved with Marc's niece and nephew."

"I see," said Ashley, although she didn't. She couldn't imagine any higher priority than getting to know the children who would become your responsibility in a very short time.

"Would you object if I met them and got to know them a little better? They might enjoy helping plan their rooms."

"Suit yourself. Actually, the children will not be spending a lot of time here at Windsong. I plan to enroll them in a boarding school after Marc and I are married. Keep in mind that their rooms will be used as guest bedrooms when the children are away. For that reason, I do not want a childish theme. Something simple and contemporary will be fine."

Ashley raised her eyebrows, "I thought I saw the guest quarters near the porte-cochere."

"Yes, but you can never have too much sleeping space for weekend house parties."

Sydney led the way back across the balcony to the master bedroom suite. They turned into a mammoth room with arched twelve-foot ceilings and French doors leading to a balcony overlooking the lake.

"This room is impossibly large," Sydney observed.

With that point Ashley agreed. "It needs a feeling of intimacy. How do you feel about grouping a chaise lounge and nesting tables at one end, and a lady's desk flanked by reading chairs at the other? That would define different areas of use. A canopied king-sized bed with draw drapes at the four posters would create an air of privacy. Few rooms are large enough to accommodate such a treatment. You are very fortunate, as this one could."

Sydney pondered the suggestions. "Wouldn't that be too old-fashioned? I'll have to think about it." She glanced at her watch. "I have a luncheon appointment shortly. Do you have any further questions before I go?"

"No. I'll translate these notes into a preliminary proposal from which we can draft a contract. Shall we plan to get back together with Mr. Perone in about a week?"

The other woman pressed her lips together in a firm line.

11

"I see no point in that. As I explained earlier, Marc has delegated the project to me. And about the matter of a contract—they really are so cut and dried—don't you think? I prefer a more flexible working arrangement."

Ashley summoned a smile she hoped would reassure her client as they descended the stairs. "Clauses can always be added to the contract to make changes where necessary. As for Mr. Perone's involvement, his signature on a contract is a legal necessity. I'm sure you understand that I can't order structural changes to the house without the consent of the property title holder."

Sydney's black eyes snapped, but her mouth forced a taut smile. "Perhaps I should have retained an established firm in Tampa that would be more concerned with customer satisfaction than with rigid business procedures."

Ashley tucked her note pad into her briefcase. "Would you like some time to reconsider before we go any further with this," she asked cooly. Although Ashley needed this job badly, doing business without the protection of a contract would be no business at all. That much she had learned from her college apprenticeship.

Sydney's stiletto heels tapped an angry rhythm against the tile floors as she went to lock the back doors. Her head was held high and arrogantly. Much as Ashley disliked her, she had to recognize that Sydney's referrals would be valuable to the future of her business. The fees from just this contract would be enough to repay the loan from her brother. But most of all, this commission would provide impressive job experience for her portfolio.

When Sydney returned her manner had become persuasive. "Naturally I can see that working with an open-ended contract would entail a greater expenditure of time on your part, so I'm prepared to compensate you with a twenty-percent bonus on completion of the job. How does that sound to you?" she smiled ingratiatingly.

Ashley was weary. "I'll think it over—and discuss the offer with the owner."

Angry spots of color appeared beneath the other woman's high cheekbones. "Be sure you also think over *this*, Miss Ames! My references will be like money in your pocket! You also should know that no one runs a successful business in this town without the good will of the business community, over which I wield considerable influence!"

Ashley leveled her direct disconcerting gaze on Sydney. "Yes, I'm aware that all you say is true, and I'm counting on your fairness as much as I'm counting on your good references."

Sydney was taken aback. Before she could retort, Ashley said, "Would it be possible to have access to the house for taking measurements and making further estimates?"

"Yes, of course," Sydney handed her a key. "I've arranged for a woman to clean the place. Also a yardman is scheduled to come later today—just in case you run into them."

"Thank you," Ashley acknowledged politely, glad the interview was over.

Ashley watched the dust from the Mercedes as it disappeared into the grove. She lifted her blonde hair from her slender neck and leaned forward into the cold air blowing from the air-conditioning vent in her car. She wished it was as easy to cool one's temper! *Whatever possessed Marcos Perone to think he needed an interior designer*, she fumed. All he needed was someone to do the leg work for his fiancée. How frustrating to have a beautiful opportunity spoiled by having to work with such a difficult person as Sydney.

Ashley sighed. She now saw clearly why experience had been so important to the heads of design houses who had interviewed her last summer. Although she had excellent grades, her lack of experience had invariably cost her a position at the established firms. She had been naive enough to think the world was just waiting for her to finish college and make her talents available!

She smiled wanly. Was she being just as naive to think she could make a go of her own shop? Her brother Brad didn't think so. He had loaned her the money for start-up costs when the Urban Renewal league offered her free shop space. It was part of their effort to redirect business from shopping centers along the expressway back into the original business district of Avon Park. She would never have risked the venture had Brad not encouraged her, pointing out that at least it would give her practical experience.

She left the clay road through the grove and turned onto the paved highway that led into town, ten miles away. By the time the road began to wind around Lake Verona at the head of Main Street, she was humming and planning her day in the shop. The mile-long mall that divided the two facing streets of stores was exceptionally beautiful this time of year. Tropical plants flourished under the attention of the local garden club. Retirees lounged on park benches reading the local newspaper. Mothers pushed their babies along the walkways beneath trees whose branches were laden with large blossoms. They looked as though ten thousand white doves rested there.

The peaceful scene reflected the peace Ashley felt in her heart! She knew that just as surely as God had planned this beautiful creation, he also had a beautiful plan for her life. During those winter months of futile job hunting in Chicago, she had thought God to be deaf. At last she had quit making childish demands on him to provide a job—and only then had God been able to work in her life. When she had come to the end of herself, she found she was at the beginning of a place called trust.

With that daily surrender to him, the thread of events had begun to weave the fabric of her life, beginning with the feature article in the Avon Park *Sun* welcoming her to the community and giving her decorating credentials good exposure. It had been unexpected publicity, and she was overwhelmed by the interest generated. Encouraged, she had accepted her brother's loan and opened her own shop, Ashley's Signature Interiors.

As she pulled up to the curb, she admired the bright blue awning scrawled with an enlargement of her own signature in white, which shaded the shop entrance. She wanted to convey that every home or place of business should express the personality of its occupants as uniquely as a personal signature.

Ashley was smiling happily as she inserted the key in the lock. The deep pile of the cinnamon-colored carpet cushioned her feet as she walked through the shop switching on the lamps in the recessed cubicles that lined the soft beige walls. Ashley straightened the magazines in the hospitality center and took the tea tray to the work room to make a fresh brew.

The wind chimes near the front door tinkled and a cheerful, slightly breathless voice called, "Hello? Anybody home?"

"In here. Come on back, Beth Ann."

Her green eyes questioning under feathery brown bangs, Beth Ann plunked her lunch down on the work table. In her usual forthright manner she asked, "Well? How did it go?"

Ashley made an iffy hand gesture. "So—so. O.K., I guess."

"What did you think of Marcos? Did he give you the contract?" Beth Ann asked as she unwrapped a sandwich. She had a vested interest in the time and talent she had spent helping Ashley set up shop, and she felt nearly as involved as the owner herself.

Ashley poured them both a cup of tea. "As a matter of fact, Mr. Perone didn't keep his appointment. Sydney Ogleby did." Beth Ann's mouth fell open, then she said half angrily, "What on earth was *she* doing there?"

"He asked her to coordinate the redecorating of Windsong."

Beth Ann was still puzzled. "It's been rumored that Sydney spends a lot of time at his apartment, but I just assumed she was helping him settle his family estate since she works in the trust department at the bank."

Dryly, Ashley said, "When a woman decorates a man's house for him I'd say their relationship is more than business."

"Obviously. I just thought Marc would have better sense than to get involved with her, especially since he has a niece and nephew to care for."

"Well, since I have never met the illustrious Marcos Perone I can't pass judgment on his choice of Sydney for a—whatever. I *have* met his house and I've fallen in love with it. I just hope I can negotiate the contract effectively. Sydney and I have quite different ideas and she seems unwilling to have me discuss the project with Marcos." She took a bite of apple wedge. "But that doesn't mean I'm not going to!"

"Good girl. Don't let Sydney intimidate you. She uses that snob routine on everyone—and usually gets by with it, unfortunately."

Beth Ann brushed the crumbs from the table into her hand and said casually, "Howis is driving over from the Cape this afternoon. It seems that he and some of his friends have planned a get-together at the country club this evening."

"Sounds nice." Beth Ann adored her brother, a chemical engineer at Cape Canaveral.

"He's bringing a friend who's licking his divorce wounds. I'm supposed to go to the country club with him and dance his troubles away." She flung her arms to her side hopelessly. "Why do I always get the ones who are only looking for their bruised egos to be massaged?"

"Maybe it's because of your soft touch," Ashley laughed.

"Well, the only reason I agreed to go is because I haven't had a date since last New Year's Eve—and that one was stuffed with olives on an hors d'oeuvres tray. Yuck."

Ashley broke into laughter. "Sounds about as palatable as some of the dates I've had!"

"Don't laugh so fast," warned Beth Ann. "I told Howis you'd go with him, because I'm not about to be one of a threesome."

"Beth Ann! I'll do nothing of the kind! You know I don't go out with blind dates."

"My brother is not a blind date, thank you," sniffed her friend. Her eyes began to twinkle. "He has twenty/twenty vision where beautiful women are concerned." She smirked and said, "Besides, Marc is going to be there. In fact, the party is for him, kind of. Howis called him from the Cape and persuaded him to leave business long enough to get together with some of their college fraternity brothers."

Beth Ann was right. A social event would be the perfect excuse to meet the man she had practically been forbidden to contact.

"O.K., Beth Ann. What time tonight?"

"Good girl," Beth Ann chortled. "I knew you'd see it my way."

Ashley made a face and walked with her to the door.

Ashley spent the afternoon unpacking exquisite glass accent pieces and displaying them on the lighted shelves. Business was steady and there were several purchases of watercolors placed on consignment by a local artist. One customer even ordered a house full of custom draperies. Ashley had been fortunate to find a local seamstress who did professional work. The woman also stitched toss pillows, a happy addition to the accent inventory of the shop.

By five o'clock Ashley had totaled her tickets, recorded the sales, tidied the shop, and was ready to leave. Even though she loved the shop, she always felt

17

as though she was going on vacation when she started out to her grandfather's cozy lake cottage, just on the far side of Lake Verona. On the way she waved to Beth Ann's mother who was in the yard of her mobile home. She had been the first person Ashley had met after moving into the cottage. Mrs. Brody had come over to welcome her and to express her regrets at her grandfather's death some months before.

The late afternoon air was sultry and hotter than midday when she entered the cottage. Ashley had two hours to spare before she needed to dress for the dinner party at Pinecrest Country Club.

Suddenly she decided to go out to Windsong and begin taking measurements. The sooner she put a proposal and cost estimate together, the sooner she could collect a retainer fee on a contract. She slipped a T-shirt on over her blue jeans, tied back her hair in a plaid scarf, and grabbed her briefcase on the way out.

Ten minutes later she was turning onto the packed clay road that took her deep into the fragrant groves. Again she was struck by an eerie sense of isolation.

This time she drove into the porte-cochere and let herself in the side door to avoid the overgrown front yard. Taking her pencil, note pad, and measuring tape from her briefcase, she set about systematically getting the data she needed. Time was forgotten, so deep was her interest now that she could explore with leisure.

Curious about the wood in the staircase carving, she found an old cloth in the kitchen and began to rub away flaking paint to bring up a patina. Distant thunder sounded, but she paid no attention. It was not until a much louder rumble that she looked up and saw that part of the roar had been a jeep's engine. Startled, she was glad she had made sure all the doors were locked when she came in.

A tall bronzed man vaulted over the side of the jeep and began to unload bulky burlap sacks—the yardman Sydney had spoken of, no doubt. The muscles of his bare shoulders rippled as he slung the heavy load across them. His bare chest was broad and thickly matted with curling hair. He strode to the portico where he stacked the sacks, handling his load with ease. On the trips back and forth to the jeep, she saw him eyeing her car with curiosity and she shrank down behind the staircase.

When he finished unloading, he turned toward the house and strode purposefully to the front door, his lean hips defined by close-fitting, blue jean cut-offs. Ashley's breath came in quick spurts as she tried to decide whether to answer the door if he knocked. She trembled, realizing it had begun to get dark, and she was so alone!

He peered in the glass beside the door, just as she had done only that morning. She caught a glimpse of his stern face with its stubby growth of beard. He knocked at the door and when no one answered began to rattle it fiercely. Ashley slunk farther up the stairs, not sure if she should try to hide or make a dash for her car.

"Hello? Who's there?"

His voice vibrated with a deep power, yet there was a refined edge to it she certainly didn't expect from a yardman—although having never met one, she wasn't at all sure how he was supposed to sound. She muffled a hysterical giggle.

With all the valuable paintings and sculptures around, she dare not answer the door to a stranger. He called again. A deep excitement arose within her at the timbre of his voice.

He made his way to the back flagstone terrace on the lake side of the house. Ashley lost no time scurrying the rest of the way up the stairs. She crouched low so he couldn't see her.

His striking figure came into view and took an aggressive stance outside one of the long arched windows. Ashley caught her breath. With arms folded against his broad chest he looked like a Viking.

Raising his voice several decibels, he thundered a

warning punctuated by angry oaths. Ashley shivered. She certainly wouldn't want to encounter him in this state. He motioned wildly to the sky, slammed his fist against one of the window frames, and finally stomped off. Shortly, she heard the roar of an engine as the jeep left the grove.

Ashley breathed a sigh of relief and gathered her belongings. She was more than ready to leave. She noticed for the first time the boiling black clouds over the lake. She wasted no time getting into her car and heading out of the grove. The first raindrops began to pelt her windshield before she was even out of sight of Windsong. Slashes of lightning cut through the dark clouds. The raindrops soon became a torrent, making it impossible to see the road ahead. She switched on her headlights and drove doggedly on, hoping to reach the highway before the clay road became impassable. Already the deep ruts were puddled and the surface slippery.

Lightning gave a brief, daylight brightness to the grove before plunging it into total darkness again. Uneasily, Ashley slowed. As she did, the wheels spun and the car began to slide crazily. She wrenched the steering wheel and braked. The car lurched, and the helpless feeling of having no control came over her. She instinctively braced. After a series of bumps and thuds, the car came to a stop in a ditch beside the road, mired in a sea of thick mud.

Ashley took several deep breaths to control her shaking. Timorously, she shifted gears and pressed the accelerator, although she knew it was usless. There was a high whining sound as the engine tried vainly to move the car.

"I'm stuck, but good!" she muttered disgustedly. "And probably for the night."

She laid her head back against the seat. Hot tears stung her eyes. Too late, she at last understood the man's loud warnings. Would she ever grow accustomed to the sudden changes in this tropical climate? Muggy heat nearly always meant a squall was on the way.

There was no letup in the cloudburst. Ashley squirmed in the uncomfortable small space. High winds rocked her car. She moaned. She hadn't even told anyone where she was going, so there was no hope of anyone coming to look for her. She quaked at the thought of spending the night alone in the grove. If this was what it meant to be on your own, then independence was certainly not all it was cracked up to be, she decided.

When she looked up again, two blurred circles of light were coming toward her. Panicking, Ashley began to blink her own head lights to signal the other vehicle. It drew close and she recognized the same jeep that had been at Windsong earlier. The same thunderous voice bellowed, "I figured you'd get stuck in the mud, all right! Get in the jeep!" he ordered, jerking his head toward the empty seat beside him. She fumbled with her lights while he yelled for her to hurry. She stepped knee deep into the swirling ditch of water. The downpour drenched her in a moment. The wind grasped her hair and flung it in her face as she struggled to the road. He had the door open, waiting. A strong arm reached out and hoisted her up into the jeep.

"I forgot my keys!"

"Never mind! No one is going anywhere with your car tonight, I guarantee you," he growled as he put the jeep in gear and began to back it around.

She took one look at the angry face of her rescuer and fear struck her heart. Chilled, she began to shake all over.

He reached under the driver's seat and brought out a flask. "Have some. I keep it for just such emergencies."

She shook her head. He shrugged and stuck it back under the seat.

His dark brown eyes traveled the length of her shivering form. "There's a blanket in the back you can wrap up in."

She resented his imperious attitude. "No thanks."

"Suit yourself." His eyes scanned the curves of her body, molded clearly under the wet clothing.

She blushed and reached for the blanket.

He concentrated on the road ahead of him. Ashley noticed he handled the Jeep expertly, in command of it as he obviously expected to be in everything. She noticed the hands on the steering wheel were well-manicured. While strong, they were not the work-roughened hands of a gardener. He obviously spent time in the sun, judging from the deep tan on his bare chest. The thick sun-bleached hair fell in loose waves and was neatly trimmed at the base of a strong muscular neck encircled by a gold chain. What a paradox for a man who wore ragged cutoffs and shabby sneakers!

The man muttered as the jeep hit a deep rut and careened sideways. He glared at her. "You could have saved a lot of trouble if you had left when I told you to. The cleaning chores could always have been finished later!"

So he thought she was the cleaning lady, did he? Suddenly she remembered her appearance. No wonder he thought she was the domestic help. And he probably had seen her wipe off the handrail. Well, let him think it. He probably wouldn't believe her anyway if she told him she was an interior designer. She stifled a giggle.

Still angry, he growled mercilessly. "Anyone with common sense would have known to get out of the grove before a squall. Why didn't you come to the door when I called?"

"No one asked you to come back for me," she shouted. "If it's such a bother to you, just stop and I'll get out right here!"

For a moment she thought he was going to do it. Instead, he said sarcastically, "Now that's gratitude for you!"

They lapsed into a hostile silence, and Ashley was

22

glad when they turned onto the highway. Almost as though Mother Nature was pulling tricks on them, the rain stopped as suddenly as it had started. The sun appeared on the horizon for one final burst at the day. *It's infuriating that so short a rain shower can cause so much trouble*, she thought darkly. She'd have to call a tow truck to get her car out of the ditch.

The two maintained a stony silence all the way into town.

"Tell me where you live and I'll take you home if it's not too far. I have an engagement this evening that I'm running late for."

"Just drop me at the drugstore," she said through gritted teeth. "I have a friend who'll come for me."

"Fine!" He stomped on the brakes and brought the jeep to the curb.

Ignoring the hand he offered to help her down, she sprang to the ground.

"I suppose I should thank you," she said tersely, unaware that her patrician nose had tilted and that in her bedraggled state she looked like a miffed kitten.

With an amused glint in his eyes the man said evenly, "I suppose you should."

She flung a bill on the empty seat. "I reserve my thanks for those who are civilized enough to understand the meaning of the word!"

She heard him laughing as she fled to the pay phone and called a taxi.

Chapter Two

In her bathroom at the cottage Ashley removed her soggy clothing and sank gratefully into a tub of hot water foaming with bubbles. Now that the incident was behind her, she was slightly ashamed of her behavior. She admitted the man's rudeness was little more than aggravation, understandable in the circumstances. He came often to her thoughts. His liquid brown eyes seemed permanently etched on her memory.

She patted herself dry with the fluff of blue towel, then folded it around her like a sarong, and began to work on her hair with a blow dryer and hot rollers. On the one hand she was looking forward to an evening at Pinecrest. It was a local resort country club reputed to have one of the best cuisines in south Florida. For the most part the club catered to 'snowbirds' during the winter. The crowds were so heavy that the locals preferred to patronize it in spring and summer when the tourists had gone home.

On the other hand, she hoped Howis Brody was not going to be a problem. According to Beth Ann he was about the best thing walking, but Ashley knew her friend adored her brother and probably had exaggerated.

Her thoughts drifted off, again to the eyes of her dark, handsome rescuer. She was suddenly aware that those eyes had been with her since they parted. He lurked in the shadows of her mind like a welcome intruder.

She slipped a pale pink dress over her curved form and adjusted it before the full-length mirror. The simple dress had superb lines with a draped neckline that formed cap sleeves over the shoulders before it plunged into a deep curve at the small of her back. The soft, shell pink cast a glow over her creamy complexion. Eye shadow gave a brilliance to her deep blue eyes framed by long curved lashes.

Ashley smoothed on the silvered sheer hosiery and stepped into silver sandals. Looking critically in the mirror, she decided the dress deserved a gala hairstyle. She swept her blonde locks to one side and pinned loose curls here and there, allowing some to trail over her ears and at the nape of her neck. A spray of tiny, pink silk flowers added a romantic, whimsical touch. Pearl earrings, a touch of lipstick, and a musk fragrance created the final magic. Ashley picked up her silver evening purse and went into the living room to await her guests.

She switched on the gleaming brass lamps and sat on the blue-and-white houndstooth loveseat which matched the cottage curtains. This was the room her grandfather had loved so much. A chiming clock stood on the mantle, flanked with pots of ivy. A hooked rug covered the polished hardwood floor. Ashley had recently hung baskets overflowing with ferns and tossed bright yellow and white accent pillows about to brighten the room.

Tigger leaped up beside her looking for the gentle strokes he knew his mistress would give. Her long fingers caressed the calico cat that had appeared with the paper one morning.

She scratched Tigger's head and smiled at his contented purring. A few days ago he had led a hapless existence, then he had found someone to trust and a place to belong.

"I envy you, cat," she whispered and drew the kitten to her cheek. It was a gesture of loneliness. She thought of her own parents' comfortable relationship, and of Brad and his wife who were still building theirs, and somehow felt left out. She eyed the phone, and impulsively decided to share the good news with Brad that she had landed her first account. After all, he had loaned her the money to open the shop—she'd like him to know there was hope of getting it back!

He answered the phone, and Ashley bubbled over with her news. "So you see, I should be able to send you a check the moment I receive my first installment on the fee."

"Well, if you're sure—but I'd like you to send it to me at the office. Don't send it to the house."

His voice was so positive Ashley exclaimed in surprise. "Brad! Does Paula know you loaned me the money?"

"There was no reason for her to know."

"That isn't true. You and Paula always share everything." Ashley hesitated, deciding whether to press the point.

Brad said, "Paula has been going through a bit of a problem, Sis. She just isn't herself these days. There's no reason to worry her with unnecessary concerns. She'll be O.K." His voice was gruff with emotion and he didn't sound as sure as he had intended.

"Have you heard from Mom and Dad this week?" asked Ashley, sensing it was time to change the subject.

Brad chuckled. "Europe will never be the same. Dad got some time off from classes and they toured the Alps. Mother was ecstatic over the wildflowers. She probably took a million pictures."

Ashley smiled and her eyes misted with tenderness. "This sabbatical was so good for them. They've been needing some time off together for a long while."

After a few more minutes of chatting Ashley rang off. She ran her delicate pink-tipped nails through the cat's soft fur, an unconscious frown creasing her forehead. She didn't like it at all that Brad hadn't confided in Paula about the loan. She had sensed Paula's stress when she stayed with them while job hunting. In fact, it was when she overheard an argument between them that she realized she had overstayed her welcome, and had headed for the Florida cottage.

She pursed her lips thoughtfully. Could their problems be more serious than he was letting on? If so, they certainly didn't need any added friction over a loan Brad had made without his wife's knowledge. She redoubled her determination to pay off the loan with all possible speed.

Car lights zoomed into the driveway and Ashley heard the roar of a sports car engine. It was a deliriously happy group that trooped in and Ashley was suddenly glad she had agreed to go with them.

Introductions were made, and the tall, fair-haired Howis turned to his sister and said reproachfully, "You told me she was the ugliest of the wicked stepsisters!" He grinned at Ashley and tucked her hand in the crook of his elbow. "Instead it's Cinderella I'm taking to the ball."

Beth Ann grinned smugly. "Serves him right. He told me Dave, here, makes his living as a fisherman. I've been chattering about commerical fishing for the last half hour—then Dave explained he's an aquatic research scientist and the fish he catches are lab specimens!"

They all laughed, with Dave drawing circles at his temple with a forefinger and shaking his head hopelessly.

Ashley quipped that the whole business sounded fishy to her, a pun that brought hisses and boos from the others.

A band was playing by the pool. White-coated waiters moved quietly between tables lit by torches and colored lanterns overhead. The flickering lights cast mystical shadows on the masses of flowers that grew beneath the palms.

Howis and Beth Ann took pleasure in introducing Ashley to the town's society, made up largely of professionals and wealthy retirees. The brother and sister had been quite frank about their own status in this small town society. Their parents had been respected for their high principles, but had never moved in the same circles as the country club set. Only since Howis had made it as a master chemical engineer at Cape Canaveral had he been invited to join Pinecrest Country Club.

"At the time it seemed important to me because it was a goal I had never achieved," he explained as he and Ashley sat together at a small table. His face assumed a slightly scornful expression as he continued. "It means nothing to me now except as a place to meet friends when I occasionally come home."

Ashley remembered Beth Ann saying that they had been reared in the superintendent's house on the Perone estate. Howis and Marcos had been inseparable growing up, and Marc had been as much at home in the Brady house as in his own. Beth Ann's loyalty to Marcos was almost as strong as her loyalty to her own brother.

Ashley looked across at Howis. He was attentive and easy to be with, ruddy of complexion with a ready smile. There was a relaxed assurance about Howis. He was a Rock of Gibraltar type. They discussed his work and her work, and after that there seemed to be little to say. Soon he excused himself to greet a friend across the room. As he walked away, Ashley suddenly realized she had been secretly hoping he would turn out to be a prince charming. *How unfair of me to put that kind of expectation on anyone*, she thought to herself. Would she ever outgrow that little girl fantasy of some day meeting a man who would make her pulses thunder? Dreamily, a sun-bronzed head and careless roving brown eyes came to her mind.

Ashley had not seen Sydney come in, but there she

was by the buffet at one end of the pool. She was stunningly elegant in simple black. The sleek cap of raven-black hair had been transformed into expertly coiffed windswept curls. A small white orchid nestled over one ear, giving just the right touch of glamour. Ashley felt pale by comparison to Sydney's exotic beauty, unaware that her own fragile peaches-and-cream beauty brought her admiring glances from these darkened native sun-worshipers.

Sydney joined Ashley. "My dear! How nice to see you!" She touched her cheek to Ashley's.

Startled, Ashley stepped back. Could this be the same woman who only a few hours ago had treated her with contempt?

Lifting a heavily bejewelled hand, the woman in black signaled across the room to her escort. He sauntered toward them, glass in hand, wearing his dark evening attire with casual confidence. The dark tuxedo set off his athletic physique and deep tan.

"Marc, darling! I want you to meet our decorator. She has the most marvelous plans for Windsong!"

Ashley scarcely heard the introduction as her gaze collided with the piercing brown eyes. In one electrifying moment she took in the shock of sun-bronzed hair, the straight nose and the square jawline.

She closed her eyes, refusing the truth. It was the man who had rescued her from the storm—and he was none other than Marcos Perone, wealthy citrus grower and her first client!

Ashley held her breath. Perhaps he wouldn't recognize her. After all, she hardly looked like the scrub woman he had rescued. One look at his penetrating smile and the sardonic gleam lurking in the corner of his eyes, and she knew he remembered. Color rose to her cheeks as he laughed softly.

Sydney seemed oblivious to all this as she tucked both hands into the crook of his elbow and chatted about the new look Ashley was going to create for Windsong.

Marcos frowned and looked slightly puzzled. "Not too new, I hope."

"Oh, no, darling," Sydney interjected quickly and cast a warning glance at Ashley. "Just a few changes here and there."

A group of newcomers came and swept them away. Ashley was alone for a moment. She caught her lower lip between her teeth thoughtfully. A few changes here and there hardly described the radical renovation Sydney had in mind for Windsong. Caution reminded her to proceed carefully.

Howis returned and slipped an arm around her waist. "Have you had punch? Let me get you some. Then there's an old friend I want you to meet."

And so once again Ashley faced those deeply penetrating brown eyes. When Howis started to make introductions, Marc shot Ashley a curious smile.

"We've already met—*twice*," he emphasized dryly, and turned his attention to Howis.

"They tell me you're the brain behind the new chemical combustion system for the XXI missile. Tell me, how did you make the change to space chemistry? You've come a long way from agricultural formulas."

Howis grinned. "As always—I never could sneak past you on anything!"

As the two continued in conversation Ashley drifted toward the fountain, admiring the tropical fish darting about under its flow. She stood gazing into the depths. Was Sydney deliberately deceiving Marc? Was her blasé denial meant to disguise her real intentions? For the second time that day Ashley had a queasy feeling she was getting caught in the middle. She was startled by a voice behind her.

"Not thinking of jumping in, are you?"

She whirled and confronted a pair of shrewd black eyes that somehow didn't match the jovial voice.

"If you are, you wouldn't be the first. These dinner parties usually end with dunkings in the pool after the champagne starts running at high tide."

Ashley laughed. "Maybe it *is* a good way to sober up if that's what they need!"

"It's usually just a bunch of old college buddies who try to recapture their youth," he chuckled. "Silly, but harmless." The short stocky man introduced himself as Stan Wittmore, the corporate attorney for Perone Enterprises.

"I believe you and Sydney are working together on Windsong." She nodded and he continued, "A fascinating place. Has anyone told you how it came by that name?"

She shook her head. "No, but I'm interested."

He hesitated and seemed lost in thought. "The name resulted from a tragedy, actually. The first generation of Perones had just built and moved into one wing of the mansion. In those days predicting hurricanes was guesswork. Señor Perone had only a few hours warning to get as much of the fruit crop picked as possible. Storms don't usually come as late as December after the fruit is ripened, but this one did. He was out with his pickers until the storm hit. Señora Perone was left with the five little ones to weather the storm. She kept them entertained by listening for the songs of the wind whistling through the young Australian pine windbreaks."

Ashley nodded. She had seen the towering straight rows of pines surrounding the grove, but had no idea they were a powerful curtain to break the impact of winds that would otherwise pound the fruit right off the trees.

Stan went on. "Señora Perone dozed off but was awakened by the youngest child crying that the wind had stopped singing. Realizing that the silence was a deadly one, she gathered her brood into the hallway, and threw feather mattresses over them just in time. A killer tornado descended out of the hurricane and

31

ripped the house away. When Señor Perone rushed home, he found his family, hands clasped, singing a wind song about triumph over the storm. Out of that tragedy came a beautiful folksong—the wind song. Grove workers sang it for years, then gradually it became lost."

Ashley pressed a finger to her misty eyes. "What a shame. I would have loved to have heard it." She paused, then said almost reverently, "I knew there was something special about Wingsong the minute I saw it. That really should be the theme of our lives, shouldn't it? In every wind of life, a song."

Behind them there was the sound of soft applause. "Beautifully said," Marc commented quietly. "I hadn't remembered that story in years, nor have I heard such meaning put to it."

He turned to Stan. "Excuse us, Stan. I want to show Ashley the garden."

With a hand at her elbow he guided her away from the crowd and onto a cobblestone path through the lantern lit gardens.

"Since we have now been properly introduced—twice—I think we can assume we're safe in each other's company," he grinned, casting a sidelong glance to measure her reaction.

"If you had introduced yourself at our first meeting instead of trying to break the door down like a hoodlum, we could have avoided the very inconvenient consequences," she said pertly.

He raised his eyebrows. "On the other hand, you might have come to the door long enough to find out who I was, instead of behaving irrationally."

She bristled. "I felt a certain responsibility for the valuable paintings and sculpture. How was I to know you weren't some vagrant intent on marauding the place?" She wanted to add that he had certainly looked the part.

"As a matter of fact," he said grimly, "that's exactly

why I was checking you out. Sydney had said she was sending a lady to clean, and—" he hesitated.

"And you thought I was the cleaning lady and might lift some of the family silver," Ashley finished for him.

He grinned. "Something like that. I saw you dusting the hand rail to the stairs and on your knees scrubbing at the tile, so it was a natural assumption." He paused and quizzed, "What *were* you doing?"

"I was examining the condition of the tiles."

"And?"

Ashley took a deep breath. He had asked, and whether Sydney liked it or not, she was going to give her honest assessment.

"And they are in excellent condition considering their age. They are hand painted tiles. A ceramist could be able to duplicate the few that need to be replaced."

Marc grunted and nodded approval. Ashley wondered if she dare bring up the arched leaded windows that were in danger of being replaced. She decided not to press her luck too far. Sydney might forgive one slip, but two would seem an obvious effort to undermine her plans.

They fell silent and walked among the gerberas, nasturtiums, and lilies. The air was fragrant with night-blooming jasmine.

Inexplicably, Ashley's steps seemed feather-light as she drifted along beside Marc's definite stride. There was a heady magic in the evening that made her want to embrace the moment.

Marc studied her from beneath deeply hooded brows. Even in the darkness she could feel the warmth of his gaze and faltered, becoming suddenly self conscious.

"What is it, Marc? Is there something else—?"

"I'm just wondering how I ever mistook you for the cleaning lady." His eyes swept appreciatively over her pink-clad figure.

She laughed. "I suppose I have come off a little bit

33

like Cinderella. Believe me, I don't always go to work dressed as the wretched stepsister. I suppose it was a pretty good April Fool's Day joke on us both."

The glow from the lanterns bronzed Marc's smiling face. "Well, I wouldn't want to be the fool twice today, and I would be if I didn't kiss the fairest princess at the ball." He drew her into his arms and lowered his head toward her. Tremulously, she braced her hands against his shoulders to stop him.

They were startled by the sound of music from the patio as the band began playing the last set for the night. Marc's arms dropped to his side as she pushed back.

"Sydney will be looking for you," Ashley said breathlessly.

With a quirking smile he led her back and quickly scanned the group at poolside.

Suddenly, Sydney's voice trilled up Ashley's spine. "There you are, darling! Stan and I wondered what had become of you!"

Marc greeted Sydney warmly and she darted him a welcoming smile that chilled Ashley's heart.

"That wasn't exactly the smartest maneuver you could have made," Stan growled in her ear as Marc and Sydney moved away.

"What do you mean?" Ashley asked, genuinely confused.

"Sydney won't take kindly to being publicly embarrassed by you. Half of the people here saw you and Marc leave for your romantic moonlight stroll. And you can believe they kept watching for your return!"

"Really? Are they always so interested when business acquaintances talk a little business?"

"Save it for the funny papers, Ashley! Everyone here knows Marc well enough to know he doesn't talk business on a moonlit garden path. He may have changed— but not *that* much. It has always been his modus operandi to charm the newest belle of the ball."

"Stop it, Stan!" Ashley snapped, bright spots of color warming her cheeks. She glanced across the pool at Sydney and Marc, their arms entwined about each other's waists. Ashley felt loneliness wash over her even stronger than she had sensed earlier at home. She saw Stan's thick lips move without hearing what they had to say. Resolutely she marshaled her concentration. He was inviting her to a cocktail party at his apartment a week from Saturday.

"I'm not much on that, sorry."

He said coaxingly, "Marc will be there."

"So?"

"I'd guess you would probably enjoy a few more of these—ah—business talks? It's always good business to get to know the boss on social terms."

"Marc isn't my boss. I'm my own boss."

Stan laughed. "Don't kid yourself, honey. Everyone who works for him answers to him fully, even if they are only on a contract."

Ashley groaned inwardly. She probably would *never* get Sydney to sign a contract. Should Marc ever be difficult, she'd have nothing to back her up. Maybe Stan was right. She should see Marc as often as possible to keep the lines of communication open.

"What time?" she asked.

Stan grinned smugly. "Good girl. Come around seven. Then we'll all go out to dinner later."

Howis joined them and complained that he hadn't seen her for the last hour. Ashley gratefully let him lead her off in search of Beth Ann and Dave.

Back at her lake cottage Ashley accepted the courteous kiss from Howis in the spirit it was given—one of good camaraderie and friendship.

"I'll be back in town next weekend. I'd like to take you to the Chalet Suzanne in Lake Wales for Chateaubriand. Are you free Saturday evening?"

"Oh, it sounds wonderful, Howis, but I've already agreed to go to Stan's cocktail party."

He raised his eyebrows. "Now that surprises me. Stan's cocktail parties could be more accurately described as drunken orgies."

"Really," she frowned. "Well, I don't really regard it as a party. To me it's business. Stan said if I'm going to work with Marc I should get to know him on a social basis and this would be a good opportunity."

Howis shook his head. "I doubt Marc will even be there. He usually steers clear of Stan's shindigs."

Ashley's heart plummeted to her shoes. "Thanks, Howis."

"Let me know if you change your mind. The offer is open."

Ashley rode to work with Beth Ann the next morning. When she walked out to the little VW Beth Ann was making all kinds of ridiculous faces.

"It's not fair that you always look like a fashion model while the rest of us suffer with freckles, fat, and phoney eyelashes," she moaned, scanning Ashley's simple blue shirt-waist dress. Its tailored look gave way to provocative side slits.

"You aren't fat," Ashley protested. "You're just a couple of inches too short for your weight! Your freckles go with your pixie personality, and there's nothing wrong with phoney eyelashes. We all do what we have to do to impress our public," Ashley grinned, "particularly of the masculine gender."

"Well, just the same, all the men look at you, while the rest of us win the Miss Dowdy of the Year award!"

Ashley made a face back at her. "Don't be so hard on yourself, Beth Ann. You're a nice person. That counts more."

"But how is a man ever going to know that if he never gets around to asking for the second date?"

Sensitive to her friend's mood, Ashley said, "I take it things didn't go well last evening?"

Beth Ann shook her head, eyes shiny with unshed tears. "Dave looked at everyone there except me. Him and his aquatic scientist routine!" she snorted. "He ogled Sydney and said that she was one specimen he'd like to put under his microscope, and he called you a mermaid and wondered if you would fit into his bathtub."

"How awful!"

"Oh, he was pretty nice, actually. He just kept making those stupid jokes because he was nervous, I think."

"Well, give it time."

"Now you sound like my mother. I'm twenty-four, Ashley. I'd make a good wife and mother, but how is anyone ever going to know that when all they're looking for is glamour?"

"Well—I can understand how you feel, but I think you're going to have to use a different strategy if you really like Dave. We'll think of something."

Ashley was surprised to see her gray Escort parked at the curb in front of her shop. It was washed and brightly polished. She waved good-bye to Beth Ann and hurried to the man waiting beside the car with her keys. A slash of white teeth showed against his black skin.

"Mr. Marc said you already paid." He held up the mud smeared twenty that Ashley had flung on the seat of the jeep.

Ashley colored. Marc always managed to put her in her place. She thanked the man, and he climbed into a waiting truck driven by another grove worker.

It was both frustrating and gratifying that today brought so many customers into the shop. Frustrating, because she wanted to get started on her presentation to Sydney. There were wallpaper, paint and carpet samples to coordinate and mount on a display board, renderings to be done, cost estimates to compute. It was gratifying though that her shop was becoming popular, but most of the women were browsers looking for ideas they could copy themselves.

"There's nothing wrong with that," Ashley said to Beth Ann over pie and coffee that evening. "It's just that time is money to me and I can't get my presentation ready while I'm spending all my time passing out free advice. Isn't there a course offered through the adult education program to help women who want to do their own decorating?"

"No. But it sounds like a marvelous idea! Why don't you do that? Think of the publicity and exposure your shop would get."

"Hmmm, that's worth a thought. Some might even become paying customers, as well as paying for the information given in class."

They talked on about the feasibility of the plan, Ashley pointing out that the back work room could be converted to a classroom. Time for working up a course of study and getting out the publicity was a main drawback.

"I'll make you a deal," Beth Ann said tentatively.

"Uh, oh! Here it comes!" Ashley chuckled. "Let me guess. You want some more help on Sunday morning with your six-year-olds in church school, and you'll give me equal time in the shop."

"Right! My, how bright you are, Ashley." They laughed, because they had first met when Ashley rescued Beth Ann in Sunday School. Beth Ann's class had been in a panic between a nose bleeder and several frightened children. Ashley had helped dismiss class and Beth Ann had been trying ever since to recruit her as co-teacher.

Ashley considered it. "Why not?"

Between preparations for the class and finalizing the presentation for the Windsong account, Ashley was kept busy over the next couple of weeks. She had not seen Marc again, but at the oddest times thoughts of warm brown eyes could send her heart reeling, and the memory of his arms often intruded in her mind.

Ashley advertised her class in the *Sun*, naming a tuition fee that would boost her income, yet be affordable for the average homemaker. She believed most women didn't use decorators because they felt overwhelmed by them. She wanted to teach them the terminology and some basic understanding of style, color, texture, shape and form—five elements of design. After her ad appeared, the phone rang every day. Ashley soon found herself with full classes, morning and evening.

In the meantime she converted the work room as a studio, and she had set up the props for the Windsong presentation in the studio when Sydney came to review the design plans. With a confidence that came from thorough preparation, Ashley made her presentation, pointing out the advantages and disadvantages of all the options offered. She suggested that Sydney take the folders of swatches and review them and the proposal with Marc before making a decision.

A week passed. Ashley waited anxiously for the outcome. She knew Sydney had been impressed with the way she conducted the presentation. She felt an inner glow and pride in her professionalism. She had done a good job. Now if only she got the contract!

Ashley was glad for the extra challenge of the classes to keep her busy. Finally the telephone rang and Sydney asked for another meeting.

Seated again in the studio, she asked, "Is there any reason for starting in the kitchen first? I'm more interested in getting on with the main rooms. Only the cook will use the kitchen."

Ashley was firm. "Since the kitchen is basically a utilitarian area and involves the most major renovation, I thought we should begin with it. That will give you more time to experiment with fabrics and colors in the other rooms."

"Very well, then." Sydney scrawled her initials across the proposal. "That should suffice in lieu of a contract," she said with a triumphant gleam in her eyes. "If it will satisfy you, I can initial my color and fabric choices later, since there are several schemes suggested."

Ashley decided to let the matter of a contract ride, since Sydney had at least initialed the proposal. Besides, time could work in her favor to dissuade Sydney from making a travesty of the house. One of the things Ashley had to determine these first few months in business was whether she could weather difficult situations—and cope with difficult clients.

With the help of God, she was doing that. It had been after a prayer for wisdom that she realized patience would be her ally. If she were patient with Sydney she would stand a better chance of gaining her confidence. From that insight had come the plan to work on the noncontroversial areas of the house first.

Chapter Three

Work started on the Windsong renovation the last Monday morning of April. Ashley hummed as she turned the small car onto Windsong Road, and grinned a little, remembering how her father used to tease her about humming when she was excited.

Cars were parked a quarter of a mile along the road before she got to the mansion. She was amazed. Several landscapers were at work on the grounds, and the place already looked different.

She smoothed her crisp mint-green and white ensemble before going inside. Her hair was pulled back into an elegant but business-like chignon and small pearls dotted her delicate earlobes.

Ashley ran her eyes curiously over a black Porsche before she skipped up the steps. She was eager to investigate the first stages of work. The door was locked and the doorbell disconnected. Hearing voices from the opposite end of the veranda where it opened into the library, Ashley crossed over and was about to knock. She hesitated when she realized the voices were angry.

Marc's heavy tones carried through the door. "That chemical has been used as a grove pesticide for years by everyone around here. What proof does the federal government have that it causes cancer?"

Lower tones answered, somewhat intimidated Ashley

41

thought, then Marc said, "I'll take it to court if I'm forced to destroy fruit on the third of my groves that have already been sprayed. In fact, I refuse to do it without having my attorney investigate the research. Go ahead and issue your court order, Mr. Fellerman, but be ready for the fight of your life. Every groveman in the ridge area uses this same spray. Most of them are fighting for their very existence against the large frozen juice conglomerates. Quite frankly, I think it bears some looking into. I must ask you to excuse me. I have a busy schedule today."

Ashley was leaving when the door was thrust open and the government agent scuttled out. She felt sorry for him after seeing the black expression on Marc's face and the hard thrust of his jaw. He saw her standing there and said curtly, "What can I do for you?"

She stammered, "Th—the front door was locked. I wasn't aware the library was occupied until I heard voices."

He yanked the door wider. "Come in, then." His tone was milder and she quickly crossed the room to go into the kitchen wing of the house.

"Just a minute, Ashley."

She pivoted. "Yes?"

"Why wasn't I advised the workmen would be starting today?"

Her mouth flew open. "I was told to coordinate with Sydney and that she would pass along whatever information was necessary to you."

"Sydney is a professional and a detailist. She would never have overlooked advising me of the work schedule had she known it."

Ashley sputtered. "Are you implying that I—"

"It's all right this time. In the future be sure that you get Sydney the word in time to advise me, or at least call my office and leave a schedule with my secretary. I sometimes use the study for private conferences, and I dislike finding the place overrun with people. The mat-

42

ter under discussion was highly confidential." His eyes narrowed shrewdly as though trying to discern how much she had heard.

Somewhat subdued, Ashley headed for the kitchen. To her discomfort, Marc followed her. At the doorway she stopped in amazement. A workman was removing part of the flooring and paneling, and an old stone hearth had been exposed. She crossed the room and knelt to read an inscription carved in the stone:

A Mighty Man of valor doth ride upon the wind.
His mercy is upon us as stormy blasts descend.
But then a song of comfort comes singing through the trees:
God is our calm in trouble, our wind song in storm's breeze.

"Oh Marc, look! It must be the wind song. The date reads December, 1811." She clapped her hands.

Marc did look, and he saw also the shine in her eyes for a symbol of faith that had outlasted time.

She turned to him eagerly. "You *do* want it to stay, don't you?"

Marc turned to the foreman. "How about it, Jess? Is there any structural difficulty in letting it stay?" Marc began to examine the old fireplace, running his strong capable hands over the oak mantle as he waited for an answer.

The old man stuck his thumbs in his overall straps. He rocked back and forth on his heels as he studied the problem. "Well," he drawled, " 'pears to me the floor was raised two feet when the kitchen got indoor plumbing. That puts the fireplace below the floor."

Marc said, "Can the floor be taken back to the original level?"

The old carpenter scratched his head and frowned. "Not hardly. All the plumbing runs between the two floors."

"Where else could the plumbing go?" Ashley asked quickly.

The foreman looked at her as though she must be out of her mind to make such a fuss about an old fireplace. He waved a hammer at the old structure. "Don't you see how it's beginning to lean? Probably there's a crack in the foundation. It would have to be shored up from underneath."

"Yes," agreed Ashley, "that would be a good idea."

The old man spat disgustedly in the rubble. "I didn't come out here to do that job. My job is to tear out the kitchen cabinets and replace them like it says on this here plan. I only tore up that section of floor to inspect the plumbing. If you want to get someone to fix the fireplace, that's your business, but I can't hold my men up waiting on that. We got other jobs to go to."

Ashley turned to Marc. "Given some time, I know I could work something out."

Marc made a quick decision. "Jess, do what you need to do to finish up in here, but when you replace the wall and floor, be sure to leave access. Later on we can make the decision to either expose the hearth or not. No doubt Sydney would want to be consulted," he said to Ashley.

Well, that's the end of that, she thought dryly. Marc's fiancée had made it clear she had no wish to live in a museum. If she intended to remodel the house into a twentieth-century style the old hearth didn't have a chance.

Marc took his handkerchief and began to scrub away some soot. He uncovered several sets of initials scratched shallowly into the stone under the mantle. Grinning, he said, "Kids have always been kids." He began to read off the ancestral names that went with the initials. Stumped by one G. C., he went into the dining room where framed oil portraits of Perone men hung on the oval walls. Ashley followed him.

"There it is!" Marc pointed a long straight finger at a

portrait with the brass nameplate of Geraldo Carlos Perone. "As I recall the story, he was the youngest of the original family, the one who alerted his mother when the wind had stopped singing in the trees."

Ashley looked at the twinkling eyes in the old man's portrait and smiled, "Yes, I think from the mischief in his eyes he would have been the one—and I'm guessing the childlike spirit that loved the wind song in the trees remained all his life."

Marc regarded her with the probing gaze that went right to the quick of her spirit. He said, "You strike me as a very sensitive and caring woman, Ashley," then added somewhat sardonically, "If I didn't know better, you would be almost convincing."

"I hope you know, Marc, that I wasn't trying to convince you of anything. If you can't accept people—women—at face value, then you have indeed lost a great deal. Don't you do Sydney an injustice?"

Marc laughed. "Sydney would only consider it an injustice if I expected her to be a traditional woman. Fortunately, I don't. Women today have a different kind of pioneer spirit than their mothers. Instead of staying home playing pattycake with their children and chanting rhymes like "rich man, poor man," they *are* the doctors, the lawyers, merchants and organizational chiefs."

"Then somehow I'm glad that the first matriarch of Windsong missed out on all that." Ashley's eyes glimmered with humor. "Just think what a legacy of faith would have been lost to the Perone generations if she hadn't demonstrated her courage by chanting wind songs with her children."

His eyebrows shot up. "I take it you're not a proponent of the women's movement?"

"Not so. I just think that women have always had certain rights. The right to fulfill our potential and become everything that God wants us to be is an automatic birthright whether male or female. Why should we fight for something that's already ours?"

"A valid point," Marc glanced at his watch. "I'm meeting Sydney for lunch at Pinecrest. If you're finished here, why don't you join us. I would like her to hear your ideas on preserving the fireplace."

"Of course." Ashley promptly accepted, glad that Marc was interested enough to pursue the subject.

When they stepped outside, he saw that her car was blocked by several cars belonging to the workmen and said, "You might as well ride with me. The restaurant is only a short distance and I'll drop you back here."

Seated in the Porsche, Marc directed a keen glance at her and picked up the train of conversation again. "So you don't think women should spend all their lives dutifully keeping house and having babies?"

"Oh, I think it's obviously one of our priority roles by virtue of biology. After all, who else could do the job?" She grinned impishly. "God gave us families before he even gave us the church. But his kingdom in us doesn't stop there. We were created individuals for a specific purpose in God's plan for living. We make a big deal about having more women in government, protecting women from sexual exploitation on the job. We debate their effectiveness if they try to be homemakers as well as manage careers, and completely miss the fact that this is not a twentieth-century feminist issue. God has already liberated the options for women. Deborah is a good example. God appointed her a judge over Israel centuries before the first woman was appointed to a Supreme Court position."

Amusement lurked in Marc's eyes. "As I recall the story, Deborah led her army into battle because they lacked the courage to go alone."

"Right," Ashley was surprised that he knew, "and there are several others in the Old Testament who could have won the Mrs. Israel pageant, hands down."

When they arrived at Pinecrest, Marc settled back against the seat after turning the ignition off. He searched her face for a long time, taking in the generous mouth that tilted into a smile, and the clear, beautiful eyes that returned his gaze. She felt him assessing her from head to toe as though he was satisfying a certain curiosity. At last he came around to her side of the car and helped her out. He kept his big hand at her elbow as he guided her to the entrance.

At the window table where they sat waiting for Sydney, Ashley was entranced by the picturesque view of the lake. Clouds scuttled by, their passage marked by reflections on the lake's blue surface.

But Ashley did notice the quick look of disappointment on Sydney's face when she walked through the door and saw her sitting with Marc. Ashley couldn't blame her. Who would want to share this gorgeous man with another woman, even for the lunch hour?

The waitress came just as Marc helped Sydney to her seat, and they quickly settled on an appetizer of marinated hearts of palm with fresh lake trout to follow.

The crisp white spears were surprisingly tasty. "Are they really a part of the palm tree?" Ashley asked, savoring the flavor.

"Yes," Marc explained, "the bud is harvested before it sprouts into the frond, or leaf. We native Floridians call it swamp cabbage and serve it as a vegetable. It's great cooked in big washpots, seasoned with spareribs, and served up at an outdoor fish fry—right Sydney?" He called her attention back from looking over the luncheon crowd.

"Not me, darling. I like to eat in a more civilized manner."

Ashley said timidly, "I noticed several varieties of reptiles listed on the menu." She gulped. "Is that really what you people like to eat?"

"Rattlesnake and alligator, you mean?" Marc asked. "No, that's just a little sensationalism to horrify the tourists.

Ashley heaved a sigh of relief, to Marc's amusement.

They launched into a discussion of the fireplace and Ashley described a bricked pit arrangement which would accommodate the hearth without interfering with the existing floor in the rest of the room. Marc seemed to think her plan was viable and liked her idea of cushioning the ledge of the pit to be used as seats around the open hearth.

Sydney's smile was almost genuine as she purred to Marc, "But, of course, I'd like to have the fireplace opened up if that's what you want, Marcos." She reached over and kissed him on the cheek. "You know how I like to please you." The throaty laugh and the sensuous way she flicked the tip of her tongue over her lips left no doubt about the double-entendre.

"Perhaps we could discuss it further at Stan's party this weekend," Sydney said in an attempt to shelve the subject.

Marc clamped his jaw. "You know I don't enjoy Stan's brawls which he dignifies by calling them *parties*."

"Oh, darling, I think they are rather fun," Sydney purred. "Besides he has invited Ashley, and it would be a good opportunity to tie down a decision about the old fireplace."

Marc looked at Ashley. "Is that true?"

Ashley shook her head. "Sorry, Sydney. I called Stan this morning and told him I couldn't make it. It's just not my thing."

"But you would go if we needed to discuss business, wouldn't you?" Sydney asked meaningfully.

"No," Ashley said firmly. "Out of fairness to all, I think business decisions should be made with a clear head."

"My sentiments exactly," Marc agreed.

Then she shrugged. "I doubt that I shall spend very much time in the kitchen anyway. But darling, could we postpone making a final decision for a while? I really had thought of bricking that entire wall, and we might not be able to match the two kinds of brick."

"Of course, Sydney. There's no hurry."

Ashley had a choking feeling that this was the first of many postponements for the work on the fireplace. She suspected Sydney was somehow jealous of the historical antiquities and would like to destroy the remnants of the past.

Ashley turned to Marc and said quietly, "You must be sure to let Lita and Tony carve their initials under the mantle along with those of their forebears. After meeting them in Beth Ann's class at Sunday school, I think they'd like that a lot."

"You're not suggesting that they be taught to mutilate property, are you?" Sydney asked haughtily.

"It's hardly the same thing, Sydney," Marc said. "All kids like to carve their names on things for posterity. We'll let them each do it on their next birthday. Tony might even like to carve his father's initials alongside his own." A shadow crossed his face. It was the first time Ashley had heard him mention his dead brother.

On the way back to Windsong she could not resist relating an incident that took place in class the preceding Sunday. Tony had been asked to tell the Bible story for the day in his own words. Tony had added his own embellishment by ending the story with, "—when those pigs hit the water, it was the biggest case of deviled ham in history!"

Marc roared with delight. He brought the Porsche to a stop beside her own small car, turned off the ignition, and turned to face her. "You are an intriguing young lady, Miss Ashley Winthrop Ames—the only Sunday school teacher cum design shop proprietor of my acquaintance."

"And both by default," she laughed.

He playfully tugged at a curl that trailed over her earlobe. His eyes began to twinkle speculatively. "Tell me, what else about you might I find intriguing, Ashley?" His voice had deepened into a throaty whisper. "Do pretty little blonde Sunday school teachers ever permit themselves to become the student—say, for instance, in lessons of love?" He leaned toward her slowly, his eyes teasing.

She laughed at his unabashed nonsense.

"Only in the library at two o'clock on Sundays," she quipped.

"Not exactly what I had in mind," he said dolefully. "The lessons I could teach wouldn't be from the library search shelves."

"I know, I know!" Ashley laughed.

The shop door banged behind Sydney, and the anger in her voice was scarcely controlled. "It was unforgivable of you to bring Marc in on that fireplace idea without discussing it with me first. Marcos is much too busy to be interested in such matters!"

"Then you'll have to tell him that," Ashley said pragmatically. "The luncheon meeting was his idea, not mine."

"You should have told him you had another appointment."

Ashley looked at her levelly. "But I didn't."

Sydney was speechless with rage. "If I chose, I could get Marc to fire you right now! I wanted a Tampa firm to begin with, but Marcos was intent on using local enterprise for the good of the community!"

"I assure you I had no intention of upsetting you, Sydney; however, if you wish to hire another decorator perhaps that would be best for everyone concerned. A home is a very personal matter and I'm not sure our views are close enough to work together."

Sydney went rigid with fury. "How dare you speak to me that way!" All at once she cooled and a gleam came into the her dark eyes. "I warn you, Ashley, don't work at cross purposes with me or you'll be sorry."

Before Ashley could answer, a customer came into the shop. Sydney turned on her heel and left.

Chapter Four

It was almost closing time at the shop when Beth Ann stuck her head in the door. "Howis is home and we're cooking out. Mom said to invite you to eat with us. How about it?"

"Love to!" said Ashley. "Six?"

She drove to her cottage and changed into light blue shorts with a matching frilled halter. It contrasted nicely with the light tan she had acquired, giving her peaches-and-cream fairness a healthy glow. At the last minute she grabbed her white knit bikini and cotton-lace beach jacket. She had quickly learned here in Florida a swimsuit was standard equipment.

As Ashley walked over to the Brody's mobile home, she inhaled the breeze. There was a hint of the ocean in it. Although seventy miles inland, now and then stiff breezes brought the salt air with them.

She had spent most of the morning at Windsong with the paperhangers. The drapes were hung and only the carpet and accents were needed to complete the master bedroom wing.

Two weeks had passed, and Ashley had gone unchallenged by Sydney. Beth Ann had reported she was out of town on a banking convention in Hawaii, and Ashley decided to get as much as possible done while she was gone. Twice she had needed to confer with Marc, since

Sydney was gone, but his secretary in the Perone corporate offices had told her both times he was in Alaska on business.

Therefore, Ashley was surprised to see the black Porsche parked beside the Brody's mobile home when she walked into the yard. Her heart did three somersaults.

Steaks were on the grill, and Beth Ann, Howis, and Marc were in the water with motorboat and skis. At their shouts to join them, Ashley ran into Beth Ann's bedroom and changed into her suit. She pulled her hair into a chic fall at the back of her head.

Minutes later she tiptoed in and splashed some of the lake water onto her thighs to accustom her body to the sudden cold. She saw Marc coiling the ski towrope, while Howis and Beth Ann circled in the boat. Marc was looking at her in a way that made her heart thud against her chest. Suddenly she realized that not a day had gone by that he wasn't in her thoughts.

He motioned to her. "Your turn on the skis."

She laughed and shook her head. "I've never been up on water skis. I'll watch!"

"Aha! I told you I could teach you a few things!" His eyes commanded her as he said, "Come on!"

She obeyed and allowed him to fasten the ski belt around her waist and to tighten the life jacket. His hands touching her sent splinters of warmth through her body. He lowered her into a sitting position in the water, bent her knees so the skis stood upright out of the water, and handed over the bar to the towrope. After instructions on how to handle herself when she was pulled upright by the taut rope, he signaled to Howis. The boat lurched forward, the slack ran out of the rope, and Ashley felt herself lifted out of the water into a standing position. She wobbled across the water in a half-skimming, half-skidding motion, gasping at the odd sensation. Then her skis hit the wake from the boat, and she lost control, tumbling into the wash.

Howis and Beth Ann circled back to pick her up. "You O.K.?"

She nodded, sputtering, and allowed herself to be tugged into the boat.

Once back at shore, Marc said matter-of-factly, "Now go again."

Ashley refused, but he was adamant. "You can't let a tumble stop you. Keep after it." He swatted her playfully, but she saw he meant it. When she would have argued, he said, "Never set out to do something and let it get the best of you."

To her surprise, she found he was doggedly determined to have her back up on skis. His authority brooked no argument, and Ashley sensed this same spirit prevailed in whatever he set out to accomplish.

"This time, don't lock your knees. Keep them bent so you can balance your weight as needed."

She made it halfway around the lake before falling, and the third time made it all the way back to the dock before wobbling into the shallows. Her audience of three cheered.

"That's enough for today," Marc said, grabbing a towel and drying her off. "You'll be sore all over tomorrow," he grinned.

"Thanks a lot for telling me," Ashley moaned, shivering from the exhilaration and the cold water.

Marc patted her face dry with one corner of the towel then wrapped it snugly around her, knotting it above her bosom so that it fell around her like a sari. Their eyes met briefly.

Beth Ann was yelling, "I'm off," and waved as she rose expertly from the water.

"Watch her form and you'll see how it's done," Marc said. "See how relaxed she is? There's nothing to it once you get the hang of it. The boat does all the work. Beth Ann has perfect form, but then, she's been skiing all her life."

Ashley could imagine how ridiculous her own

53

clumsy efforts must have looked. "My form must have been terrible!"

There was an amused glint in his eyes. "On the contrary," he remarked, his gaze scanning her toweled figure. "I found nothing wrong with your form."

She laughed to cover her embarrassment. "Can we go shell hunting?"

It was his turn to laugh. "You might find a few mussel shells. Only the sea has seashells, Ashley!" He playfully tousled her head.

"Oh, I knew that." Ashley was disgusted with her own stupidity. "I just forgot." She was relieved when Mrs. Brody called that the steaks were ready. They ate on the patio and watched the sun drop its rays into the shimmering lake. Two egrets fluttered, then swam into the tall grass in the shallows.

"Probably the most beautiful sight in God's creation is the end of a perfect day," Mrs. Brody said.

All was quiet until Marc said dryly, "Too bad humanity had to come along and spoil it with the problems of mankind." His face darkened as though reminded of something unpleasant, and no one commented further.

After dinner, Ashley heard Marc ask Howis if the Zolfo Phosphate Mining Company was still the major producer of citrus chemical sprays. Probing further, he asked keen questions about formula changes, which grove companies were using the sprays, and whether or not the conglomerates were using the locally produced spray or bringing in their chemicals from elsewhere.

Howis said, "I don't have all those answers, but some of the chemical engineers I worked with are still around if you want me to find out."

"I do," Marc nodded gravely, "and I want to know which ones have had federal inspections and if any of them had to destroy part of their crops by federal order."

"Something going on, Marc?"

Marc said grimly, "Maybe, maybe not. I'm meeting

with the legal advisory board for the Citrus Growers Association to get some questions answered, but all incidents may not have been reported by small growers." He paused. "I think some of the large conglomerates that have bought up small groves may have done so by coercion. I had three contacts from one company about to move into the Tampa area. After I refused to negotiate with any of them, I suddenly got a visit from a federal inspector claiming the chemicals used on the Lake Byrd groves and the Arbuckle Creek groves were contaminated with a carcinogenic material."

"Do you think it was collusion between federal government and conglomerates, or was it a legitimate claim?"

"I don't know. There's also the possibility the formulas have been tampered with. The particular spray we use has not changed in years."

Ashley and Beth Ann had finished clearing the table and joined the two men.

"How does it affect the local grower when the national conglomerates come in?" Ashley asked.

"Labor is affected. The large companies hire away grove hands at just enough more per hour to make it attractive. Crop prices come down because of more competitive bargaining. The conglomerates can take a larger loss by making up for it in volume. The small grove owner can't survive those odds."

"Perone Citrus Enterprises is just as big as one of the conglomerates, though," Beth Ann pointed out. "They can't hurt you, can they?"

"Not normally," Marc agreed, "but inefficiencies and failure to keep abreast of research and machine technology have cost us in terms of production. Digging into the books, I'm finding we weren't nearly as competitive as we should have been and profits are marginal. That translates to the fact that we're financially vulnerable."

"That's when the conglomerate boys like to move in

and take advantage of the independent grove owner," Howis explained.

"I'm working night and day to turn it around," Marc said, "but I'm not at all sure it can be done. The weather and the economy will have a lot to say about that." Marc addressed Howis, "I lost my grove foreman this week. He was hired by Sun Citrus while I was away in Alaska. They're paying twice the wages of a foreman. Also, my CPA went with them."

Howis whistled. "Do you think they've discovered your weak position and are gunning to make it weaker for a take over?"

"It looks that way," Marc answered grimly. "I'm going to rehire the CPA no matter what it costs. He's a wizard with figures, but careless enough to reveal my company's financial position, giving them an advantage."

"It must be very disappointing to discover employees can become disloyal," Ashley sympathized.

Marc shrugged. "It was my father and brother they were loyal to. I was the one who always got into scrapes and brought down everyone's wrath." Ashley noticed he did not seem particularly regretful.

Crickets filled the air with a night song. It was a magic evening. The air was balmy, the food superb, and the conversation stimulating. Most of all, Marc was there with his teasing smile, humor, and strength. Even his slightest touch brought an uneven rhythm to her pulse.

He stood up. "Time for a swim to work those muscles."

Ashley shuddered. "Aren't there crawly things in the lake at night?" she squeaked.

"Only a few 'gators and a water moccasin or two. Come."

"He's kidding isn't he?" Ashley appealed to Howis.

"Could be. Alligators have bred at a rapid rate since the law made them a protected species."

Marc snorted at her fears. "I used to wrestle 'gators!"

"That's because you were as wild as a bull 'gator

56

yourself, Marcos Perone!" Mrs. Brody scolded. "Ashley, stay close to the shore and there'll be no worry."

The four played in the water, diving off each other's shoulders and doing water acrobatics. Marc gave an expert diving exhibition from the lighted dock. Finally they floated lazily, slowly treading water and talking about the latest music and theater.

Car lights turned into the drive, and a woman got out of the driver's side without cutting the ignition. "Oh great! I forgot to pick Syd up at the airport!"

Marc splashed ashore and went to meet her. In the lights from the car it was clear that she was angry and he was full of remorse. Ashley could see that their embrace was far from the enthusiastic greeting of two lovers.

Ashley felt cold as Marc began to coax Sydney into a better mood. He blamed his forgetfullness on his secretary, saying she had failed to make the note on his calendar.

"You know me, darling. My life is run by that calendar and if something misses the calendar, I miss the appointment. I'll have a word with Felicia about it tomorrow." He draped his arm around her waist and hugged her close.

She smiled petulantly and said loudly enough for everyone to hear. "Knowing you, I expect you'll make it up to me before the night is over," and patted his backside in an intimate gesture that left no doubt about their relationship. Marc laughed, but Ashley sensed the embarrassment that ran through it.

As they started to leave, Sydney turned to Ashley and asked about the progress on Windsong. Ashley had hoped all evening that Marc would ask. That he hadn't made it apparent Sydney had reinforced her role as intermediary. Ashley gave a brief progress report, and Sydney asked for a meeting on the premises the next afternoon, Sunday.

Ashley hesitated. "I don't usually schedule anything for—"

"Why don't all of you come and see the work that has been done so far on Windsong?" Marc interrupted. He smiled and winked at Ashley, saying he would give her another ski lesson now that the swimming area at Lake Windsong had been cleared. Ashley caught Sydney's quick sharp look and swift intake of breath.

When they had all agreed to go to the mansion at three the next afternoon, Beth Ann went inside to make a pot of coffee. Ashley followed and went into the bathroom to shower and change back into her shorts. She was blowing her hair dry when she heard the door slam. Moments later she switched off the dryer and heard Howis in the other room.

"Marc offered me the job of business manager for Perone Enterprises tonight at a salary that's almost too good to turn down."

His mother was surprised. "But that's not your line. You're not a farmer! You're an engineer."

"Mom, you know as well as I do that I learned all the ropes from Dad when he was overseeing the groves. Marc wants me to computerize the business and get current with all the newest research. Quite frankly, I'm seriously considering it because of the challenge. The rat race at the Cape has gotten to me, and I'm about ready to let the rats have it."

Ashley walked into the room just as Mrs. Brody said, "It would be great to have you home in my declining years."

Howis laughed. "Nonsense, Mom. You'll never be on the decline. We can't even get you to *recline* often enough. You're always working."

His mother patted his hand. "Well, I *am* getting older and whether we look on it as the decline, or the incline to the Father, it will be good to have you near."

"I'll have to think about it. Marc really needs me, though, especially if he is to keep the grove enterprises.

I have the feeling that my decision will affect his on whether or not to sell out. He needs someone he can trust enough to leave for long periods while he takes care of his Alaskan interests."

"When will you know?"

"I asked him for a month to make up my mind."

This is not an appointment to look forward to, thought Ashley as she drove down the hard clay road to Windsong on Sunday afternoon. *Sydney has a way of spoiling things—or is it my own jealousy that makes me resent Sydney unfairly?*

She had never thought a man could affect her as Marc did, especially a man already committed to another woman. Ashley often wondered about Marc and Sydney. From her observation their relationship was more physical than anything else. There was no depth of communication or caring on either side, at least in public.

Marc and Sydney were already skiing when Ashley arrived. Mrs. Brody sat beside the shallows, watching Lita and Tony splash, while Beth Ann and Howis changed at the house. Ashley joined her, reluctant to intrude on Marc and Sydney. Sydney, in a red bikini which showed off her tanned curves, was doing stunts a professional skier would envy.

"Did you know she was once part of the performing ski team at Cypress Gardens?" Mrs. Brody asked.

"No, but I can believe it." Ashley was suddenly very self-conscious of her own fumbling attempts last evening.

Marc brought the boat around and yelled a greeting at Ashley as he headed toward shore. But as soon as they docked, Sydney lured Marc and most of the others inside the house. Ashley and Beth Ann exchanged knowing glances and remained behind. It was a ploy to get Marc's attention off Ashley and onto herself.

Beth Ann, childlike, was dipping tadpoles from the

water into Tony's sand bucket. Absentmindedly she noted they were the blue-tails Dave wanted for his latest study. She was going to put them in a jar and send them back to the Cape when Howis returned.

Ashley looked at her incredulously. "You wouldn't!"

"I wouldn't?" Beth Ann was puzzled.

"The only thing Howis should take back to Dave is the *information* that you've located the species he's looking for! Of course, you'll be glad to show him where it is, if he's still interested."

Light dawned on Beth Ann's face and she giggled. "So, that's the strategy, is it? We use the tadpoles for bait!"

"That's right! But when he gets here, you're going to be the lure. We'll do some interesting things with your hairstyle and make-up." Ashley began to experiment by twisting the fluff of light-brown hair into a chic top-knot. "And look for a dress that makes you appear taller and thinner than the skirts and blouses you usually wear."

"Sounds like fun," Beth Ann admitted, then she sighed. "It just seems to be a whole lot of work. I don't know if it's worth it."

"Nonsense, Beth Ann. Remember the car rental slogan? We try harder? All of us have to do that one way or another."

They stretched out on the warm sand hoping for one more shade of tan before the sun went down. Ashley opened her eyes a few minutes later when a shadow fell over her.

"Come on, lazy bones," Howis said. "Everyone's in the house waiting for the decorator to come and take bows."

"Oh, it's not to that point yet," Ashley laughed, but looked pleased nonetheless. She and Beth Ann gathered up towels and reluctantly left the white sand beach.

The cool interior of the house was a welcome

change. They entered the large ballroom through the leaded glass doors on the lake side of the house. The group gathered in the kitchen called to them. Mrs. Brody was enthralled with the effect gained by ripping out the ceiling to expose the original beams and gain a cathedral look. A slowly spinning ceiling fan featured a tiffany light globe. In the space over the cabinets, Ashley had installed backlighted panels of stained glass, giving an old world effect.

"My very favorite part is the planter window," the five-year-old Lita announced. She turned to Ashley. "Some day will you let me plant some seeds?"

"That would be nice," Ashley agreed, noticing that Marc was nodding approval. His smile warmed the whole room. The fireplace had been boarded up and Ashley carefully avoided mentioning it.

The oval silk-walled dining room was the next attraction. The silk was in such good condition it had only needed cleaning. Ashley listened, fascinated, as Marc discussed the subjects in the oil portraits, explaining their accomplishments—and misdeeds—usually with a humorous story. Niches held busts of the mistresses of Windsong. It was interesting history.

"We'll have to have Sydney's done soon," Marc smiled at her.

"Oh, darling, I'd much rather be done in oils," she said petulantly. "Perhaps I'll break with tradition."

You would, Ashley thought.

Upstairs, they walked toward the master bedroom down a long wide hallway. "This is the room where President Teddy Roosevelt stayed when he came down to go hunting in the Everglades. I think his eyeglasses are still in the library on a shelf in one of the glassed bookcases where he left them," said Marc.

Everyone gasped in delight at the lovely master bedroom, with its elegant draperies, fresh wallpaper and matted prints. Only the carpet remained to be installed.

"Oh, Ashley! This isn't it at all!," Sydney wailed.

"Isn't what?" Marc asked, quietly alert.

She looked at Marc appealingly. "This isn't the color choice I made. Oh, Marc! I did so want this room to be perfect for us."

Ashley's blood ran cold. "The wallpaper and fabrics were ordered from samples you brought in to the shop, Sydney. I'm sure they're the same. I checked the dye lot numbers myself and the pattern designs."

"No, no, Ashley. You misunderstood! The samples I brought to the shop were the ones to be returned. Remember I told you I left my choice in a folder on the bedroom mantle?"

"You said nothing of the kind."

"See? There it is!" Sydney pointed triumphantly to a folder. Inside were blue samples in the same design as the beige-mauve in which the room had been done.

"This should be simple enough to clear up," Marc asserted. "I'm sure the contract will state the exact information."

"There is no contract," Ashley said through tight lips.

She felt Marc's attitude harden. "I see," he said coldly. "Then as Sydney has evidence and you apparently have none, I suggest you change it according to Sydney's wishes."

"Oh, no, Marc! I won't have Ashley going to that expense, especially with her just getting started in business. Just leave it as it is. It really does look rather nice."

Marc smiled at his fiancée. "That's generous of you Sydney."

Ashley was seething. *I'll just bet she wants it left— because it's exactly what she ordered!*" She all but spoke the words. Somehow, she would get it straightened out later.

Carmelita and Tony scampered up the stairs to join the party and see the rooms Ashley was going to do for them.

"Ooo-oo-oo! It's so big!," Lita squealed enchantingly, her dark eyes shining, "I had forgotten."

"These were our rooms when we used to come and visit Grammy and Grampy," six-year-old Tony said.

Ashley knelt beside them and hugged them close to her. "Now we're going to fix them up to be just for you. We can have visits so that you can tell me your likes."

Carmelita reached up chubby arms and hugged her around the neck just as Marc joined them from another part of the house. Lita ran to him.

"Ashley says she's going to make our rooms 'specially nice and that we can tell her what we like."

Ashley smiled at the little girl's glee. "It's called personality decorating," she explained to Marc. "You spend a great deal of time with clients to analyze their personalities and come up with a 'home within a home' for them."

Tony grasped her hand and began swinging it. "I love to spend time with you, Ashley."

"Good! Then perhaps your Uncle Marc will bring you to the shop someday soon and we'll look through books together. We'll talk about what you like to do and afterwards we will go for an ice cream, and just have fun!"

The brother and sister fell on her with hugs and screeches of joy. Mrs. Brody called them from the foot of the stairs, and Marc swung each under an arm, hustling them away, squirming and giggling.

From the doorway Sydney questioned Ashley harshly. "Why promise them that they can help decorate their rooms when you know they'll be away in boarding school?"

Neither heard Marc's footfalls as he returned up the stairs.

Ashley made a recommendation. "The rooms could have dual sets of spreads, draperies and accents. The juvenile set could be used when they're home, and could be changed when they're back at boarding school."

"What is this about boarding school?" Marc scowled.

Sydney tucked her arm through the crook of his elbow and patted him reassuringly. "Ashley was recommending a boarding school for the children and suggested a dual theme for their rooms. Wasn't it a thoughtful suggestion?"

"It certainly is not!" He glared at Ashley. "I have no intention of sending Lita and Tony to boarding school. They've had quite enough separation from family. It surprises me you would make such a suggestion." His voice was cold.

"But that wasn't my sug..."

Sydney interrupted and said smoothly, "Of course, we won't send the children off to boarding school, Marc. It was just a suggestion, and I'm sure Ashley didn't know your feelings on the subject." She smiled.

Ashley felt like screaming! Why did Sydney manipulate the facts to make her appear guilty? To try to explain would only sound defensive, particularly when Marc was looking at her so scathingly.

Tears blinded her as she turned on her heel. Sydney's tinkling laugh followed her and, suddenly she wanted to go home.

"Leaving so soon?" Beth Ann asked in surprise as Ashley passed her and Howis on the palm court. Ashley nodded, too nearly out of control to speak.

Beth Ann said wisely, "It's Sydney, isn't it? You don't have to answer. I know it is."

Ashley sighed helplessly. "I just don't know why she implicates me when I haven't done anything to justify it. If she doesn't want me to do the house, all she has to do is say so."

"She doesn't want to fire you, Ashley," Howis said, his hands shoved deep in his pockets as he regarded her thoughtfully. "I've known her a long time. I think she wants Marc to question your credibility just enough so that she can get by with anything on you."

"But that's dishonest!" Ashley cried, flinging her hair over her shoulder in a gesture of dismay.

"Of course it is. Sydney *is* dishonest, so she's right in

character. Leaving will only make you look guilty. You've done nothing wrong. Why should you leave?"

His common sense cleared her mind. "You're right, Howis. Besides, it's not normally my habit to be rude to my host, no matter what the situation."

"There you go!" Howis embraced her approvingly just as Marc and Sydney joined them.

Marc had ordered fried chicken, rolls, and potato salad from a fast-food restaurant, and Sydney began to arrange the food. Marc was more withdrawn than usual, but Sydney played the role of carefree, charming hostess, with a word and a smile for everyone.

If she can do that on a guilty conscience, then I can certainly do it on a clear conscience, thought Ashley. When Lita and Tony called her to come and watch them dive, she went willingly, and thoroughly enjoyed encouraging their antics.

Later as they were all going to their cars, Howis handed his car keys to Beth Ann and said, "You take Mother on home. I'm going to drive Ashley. I'll walk from her place."

"Really, Howis, I'll be all right," Ashley assured him.

"Of course, you will," Howis promptly agreed as they drove down the shale road. "I just thought you might like to talk it out."

She burst into tears. "Oh, Howis, you're so like my brother Brad. I could tell him everything."

Howis grimaced. "I wish I could be more to you than like a brother, but if that's how it has to be—then that's how it has to be."

"I wish it could be more, too, Howis. I honestly, solemnly do wish!"

"So go ahead and shoot," Howis said, his voice gruff with emotion. Ashley was even more appealing when she was hurt and helpless.

She explained the devious way Sydney had twisted things to make her appear the villain. "I'm so confused

I don't know what to do. If I weren't a Christian I think I'd scratch her eyes out!"

Howis laughed. "That would be like the kitten attacking the tiger."

"Then on the other hand, if I tried to explain to Marc it would seem as though I were defensive. That's not the right approach, either."

Howis listened sympathetically. "No, it probably wouldn't be."

"Then what?" Ashley gulped back a sob, her voice pleading.

"Well, for one thing, Marc is right about the contract. You really shouldn't have let Sydney overrule you on that. Since you both now have it on good authority, I suggest you not proceed any further without one. You know now that Marc will back you on it."

"Of course, you're right. It was silly to be so anxious for the job that I let business procedures fly out the window." She paused. "Marc seems like such a fine man. I don't understand him being taken in by a woman like Sydney. He's so clever at business, surely he can read human nature better than that."

"Even good businessmen are sometimes stupid when it comes to women. I would try to explain your case to him, because I know I have his confidence, but once before I tried to set Marc straight in his romance, and I'm afraid I did more harm than good." He saddened. "Marc loved a woman named Alicia more than a man should love any woman. That's why he worked so hard in Alaska, so he could give her everything she desired when they married. She misunderstood and thought he cared more for business than for her. Out of hurt and spite, I think, she married his jealous younger brother."

"How awful for all of them."

"Yes it was. When I learned what they were planning I called Marc—but he called *me* a few choice names and told me to mind my own business. Later I learned he'd been planning to come home, but after my call he was too stubborn to be made out a fool. If I had left it alone, things might have turned out much differently."

"You couldn't have known that, and you did what you thought best."

"At any rate, I won't interfere with anyone's life again. At least now you can understand why Marc picked someone like Sydney. He would never let her get close enough to hurt him the way Alicia did. Besides, I doubt that Marc could be convinced of Sydney's manipulative strategies. He has decided to marry her, and when he gives his word, he always honors it."

"And Sydney knows that," Ashley realized bitterly. "That's why she's not afraid of her tactics being discovered."

They were almost to the cottage. Quietly, Ashley asked, "Should I go on with the Windsong project? Do you think she would try to damage my professional reputation?"

Howis parked the car and placed his hand over hers.

"I wish I knew how to advise you. You can do one thing that's certain to help—the scripture tells us, 'If any man lacks wisdom, let him ask of God who freely giveth to all men.' I think you'll be guided by his counsel in this dilemma. You know that win, lose, or draw—succeed or fail—you are the Lord's. That makes you the victor in *any* situation!"

Ashley squeezed his hand and kissed him on the cheek.

"Thanks for reminding me."

Chapter Five

Ashley held the phone away from her ear as angry invectives poured forth. She was doing her best to keep calm for the sake of the class that sat waiting before her in the studio. Ashley tried to deflect the verbal blows that bombarded her eardrums, but Marc was too furious to listen.

"It's a lucky thing for you that Builders' Supply Company called to verify the order before making the delivery and installation! Do you realize their crew was already at Windsong? They just barely reached them in time to stop the destruction of priceless, one-hundred-year-old windows!"

Ashley went white. Sydney had gone ahead with her plans, and Marc thought Ashley was responsible.

"Marc, honestly, I never ordered the fixed glass."

"And who am I to believe? The man said that Ashley Winthrop Ames called in the order and authorized it, identifying herself as the decorator of Windsong. Who but you would have done that?"

Sydney! Ashley wanted to cry out, but of course that was out of the question.

"Apparently there was a discrepancy in the amount of carpet you ordered from the same company. The salesman caught the mistake when he noticed it was tagged for the master bedroom but enough was ordered

68

for the first floor. Surely you didn't intend covering the old tiles after we specifically spoke of restoring them?" His voice was mocking.

"I didn't intend anything. These were Sydney's decisions."

His silence was as ominous as his thunderous accusations had been a moment ago.

Exasperated, she asked, "Marc, how *could* I have ordered the carpet? I would have had to go in and select the color and type. I have never been in the store.

"He said you gave him color and style numbers from a sample book in your shop."

She gave up and fell silent, which Marcos took as an admission of guilt.

"I cannot let this pass, Ashley. Mistaken color schemes are one thing, but outright destruction of valuable property is quite another. I'll see you in my office promptly at nine o'clock tomorrow morning. Please bring a final invoice of materials and fees."

In desperation, Ashley wet her lips. "Sydney—"

"Don't pass it off on Sydney," he snapped impatiently. "She knows the value of Windsong. Why would she deface it?"

Ashley longed to tell him.

"Please don't be late. I have a heavy schedule of other appointments." His voice was ice. A click sounded.

She turned slowly and faced the class, struggling to regain her composure, and wondering how much of the conversation they had figured out. Unconsciously, she squared her shoulders and lifted her chin.

"Welcome to the first class meeting of Designs for Living. I hope you will all learn enough from this course to enhance your own surroundings! We'll start by going around the table and introducing ourselves."

A dazed Ashley contrasted the light feminine voices with the deep angry tones of the man who had just destroyed her life. She had lost not only the account at

Windsong, but Marc's regard as well—and that was the greater loss. Her heart was breaking to think he could believe her careless and incompetent. She valued his good will, even though she could never have his love.

The two-hour class was interminably long. Beth Ann remained after the others had gone. "What on earth happened on the phone? When you came back you were as white as a ghost."

Ashley tried to speak, but the memory of Marc's razor-edged voice constricted her throat.

"Never mind," Beth Ann said gently. "I'll help you straighten up here, and then we'll go somewhere for a cup of tea. How about the Avalon Grill? It will be nice and quiet."

They sat in a lattice-work booth at a blue-and-white checked table. Ashley wrapped her hands around the delicate tea cup more to steady them than to warm her icy fingers.

"It was awful, Beth Ann. *He* was awful," she amended.

"Uh-oh. It could only be Marc, right?"

"I don't think I can make him understand tomorrow morning, and if I don't, he's going to fire me."

"Stop." Beth Ann ordered. "Now start at the beginning. *What* can't you make Marc understand?"

Gradually she relaxed and told Beth Ann the full story, including Marc's request for a final accounting—an unmistakable indication that she was about to be removed from the Windsong project.

Beth Ann disagreed. "I don't think Marc would do that. However mistaken he is about all this, he's still a fair man." Her calm was comforting, but Beth Ann hadn't heard the steel in his voice; she hadn't been verbally whipped.

It was hard for either one of them to believe Sydney could practice such deceit. Beth Ann traced a finger around the rim of her teacup. "Are you sure you didn't leave a business card with the company, and they just

70

assumed you placed the order?"

Ashley shook her head. "They told Marc I had given them order numbers, style, and pattern from one of the books in my shop. That could have happened. I loaned Sydney several of my carpet sample books."

The women locked glances. "There's no doubt about it, then. Sydney has set you up again. I don't know what you can do about it except pray a lot."

"Believe me, I've already been doing that!"

"Sydney never used to be this way," said Beth Ann. "Oh, she's always been spoiled rotten because she was the richest and prettiest girl in town. But she was never deceitful and unlikable until after her first marriage. Her husband was a wonderful man, the best thing that ever happened to Sydney, as a matter of fact. But he made her toe the line and didn't spoil her like everyone around her had always done. She couldn't handle it, and tried to sabotage his happiness by thrusting his children on the grandparents. She was jealous even of his attentions to them."

"She must be terribly unhappy, but somehow I don't care."

"The irony is that she's going to have the same experience with Marc. He'll never put up with her ways once he discovers what she's really like. Nor will he sacrifice the needs of Lita and Tony to keep Sydney the center of attention."

"She sounds like such a child," said Ashley.

"Exactly."

They sipped the last of their tea in silence, each aware that to say more would be vindictive.

When they parted Ashley said, "I need your prayers, Beth Ann."

"You got 'em!"

Ashley sat up most of the night preparing a contract. In a spurt of determination, she had decided she wouldn't go down without a fight. If Marc wanted a contract, she would give him a contract! She would show him she could accept justified criticism. But she didn't prepare a final invoice. She'd simply tell him it was too short notice, which was the truth. She certainly wasn't going to help him fire her.

The next morning she dressed carefully for her appointment. She chose a pale gray suit with matching gray accessories, misty hose, and pearl earrings. She coiled her hair into a severe chignon, setting off the patrician features and carved planes of her face. A touch of lavender shadow camouflaged dark circles caused by the late hours and rose lipstick disguised her pallor.

Before leaving she brewed a cup of Russian tea and sat down to compose herself. Turning to Psalm ninety-one, she read, "He that dwelleth in the secret place of the most High shall abide under the shadow of the Almighty." She read on down to verse four: "He shall cover thee with his feathers, and under his wings shalt thou trust: his truth shall be thy shield and buckler." And verse eleven: "For he shall give his angels charge over thee, to keep thee in all thy ways."

A smile came to her lips. "Thank you, Father."

She arrived at the Perone Office Building at precisely nine o'clock. She stepped off the elevator onto the plush carpets and was greeted by a smooth-mannered, smartly dressed secretary, an older woman who introduced herself as Miss Felicia Fenton.

"This way please. Mr. Perone is expecting you."

To her surprise Sydney was in the office waiting and greeted her cordially. Ashley sighed with relief. No doubt Sydney had already explained to Marc that the whole thing was a mix-up.

Marc came in from an adjoining office, his athletic frame militarily erect but moving with an easy stride. "Sit down, please Ashley." His voice was firm, his manner, stern. "I've asked Sydney to join us, as this is a matter that concerns us all."

Ashley glanced at Sydney and smiled.

Marc continued, "A mistake nearly occurred yesterday for which I can see no excuse at all. I'm not prepared to take that kind of risks any longer."

Ashley's mouth flew open, but Marc held up a restraining hand. "There is no point in denying it. Sydney tells me she knew nothing of the window order. She was quite shocked that you would violate her confidence. It was her understanding that the main ballroom was to be reserved until last, after the kitchen and bedroom wings were complete.

Ashley reeled as though she had been slapped. She could feel the color rise from the base of her throat.

Marc lifted both hands and let them fall in a gesture of despair. "What can I say, Ashley? I'm disappointed in you. Your credibility is questionable to say the least. My temper has changed since last evening, but I'm afraid my position has not."

Ashley could feel tears coming to the surface.. *"Dear God, please help me not to cry,"* she made a silent appeal.

Sydney was watching her with mocking eyes. She turned to her fiance and said laconically, "Now, Marc. Don't be too hard on poor Ashley. After all, this is her first job, and no doubt she let her eagerness get ahead of her common sense. Can't we just let it pass this time? I'm sure she'll be most careful never to let this happen again."

Marc studied his fiancée approvingly. "That's most generous of you, Sydney." The buzzer on his desk sounded, and he excused himself to take a long distance call in another office.

As soon as he was out of sight, Sydney rasped, "Good grief, Ashley! Don't take this so hard. You look like you've been run over by a two-ton truck! I'm the one who should be put out. It may take me forever to get those changes made, and in the meantime I've got to live in a ghastly museum."

Ashley nearly choked at the woman's callous admission—which she would never be persuaded to make in Marc's presence. "How can you be so unfair to me, Sydney? What if the changes had been made before the error was discovered? What then? I'd still take the rap in your place."

"I would have defended you, of course. Haven't you heard that it's always easier to get forgiveness than it is to get permission?"

Ashley stared at her aghast. "What about Marc? Doesn't it matter to you what he wants?"

Sydney grimaced. "Everybody is so concerned about pleasing Marc! What about me? Doesn't it matter what I want? After all, it's to be my home too."

"Well, I'm glad the mistake was discovered in time to prevent the lovely old windows and tiles from being ruined. I can't imagine how you've managed to convince Marc I'm responsible for this. I'm going to set the record straight the minute he comes back in this office!"

Sydney leisurely lit a cigarette. "He won't believe you."

"Why not?"

"Because he wants to believe me! Look Ashley, I know it seems like a rotten deal, but if you're going to play ball in the business world, you had better get in condition to play a tough game. I can save your job for you. In return you can help me get some of the changes I want at Windsong. Marc doesn't have to know. There are ways to make things happen."

"And why do you think I would do that for you, Sydney?" Ashley asked bitterly.

Sydney leaned back in her chair and crossed her feet at the ankles. "Because there are some things *I* can do for *you*. My father is the editor of the paper that covers the entire ridge section of central Florida. I've already asked him to do a Sunday photo feature when Windsong is complete. Now, wouldn't it be nice to have that in your portfolio? Also, in our last bank board meeting, a proposal was submitted for redoing the bank—a healthy budget is being set aside for it. I was appointed project coordinator. Would you like to have the job, Ashley?" Sydney asked tantalizingly. She narrowed her eyes and said, "I think we both have a lot to gain from a cooperative relationship, wouldn't you say?"

Ashley was stunned beyond speech. Fortunately there was no need to reply, as Marc strode into the room.

Sydney sprang to her feet and pecked a kiss on Marc's cheek. "Gotta run, darling. I have a loan closing coming up soon. Why don't we forget this little incident, hmmm? Ashley has good ideas and I really don't want to lose her."

Marc looked from one to the other as he made a decision.

"All right Sydney, on one condition. I can't allow you to be put in the middle like this again. From now on I will personally supervise Ashley so there will be no more slip-ups on the project. You've done your part and there is no reason for you to be burdened with this any longer. Since you have the wedding to plan, I imagine you'll be busy enough."

Sydney started to protest, but Marc waved her on. "See you later, sweetheart."

Sydney left, but with an expression that Ashley would have defied author or artist to capture.

Marc glowered at Ashley. "We'll work strictly from a contract—instead of the loose-ended proposals Sydney let you get by with."

"As a matter of fact I have one ready for you to look over now, Marc. You are exactly right. I was wrong to work outside a contract, and I promise that will not happen again," she said sweetly.

He seemed surprised, and took the file folder she offered. "I'll look over these and get back with you." He stood to terminate the interview and walked her to the door. "I was pretty rough on you last evening on the telephone. My apologies."

"It's forgotten, Marc."

There was a curious look on his face as he showed her out.

June came in on a heat wave. There was barely a breath of coolness, and that only in the early morning and late evening.

Ashley was spending this Saturday evening alone. She was curled up in her blue-checked living room with a book she couldn't concentrate on, Tigger on her lap. It was graduation time, and Ashley found herself caught up in reminiscences of her own graduation. Was it only last June when she took those inevitable steps into the future, leaving childhood forever behind? Pangs of homesickness assaulted her, for that was the last time she had seen her parents. They had come to her college graduation and left immediately for Europe, to enjoy her father's sabbatical from the college where he taught. Impulsively she placed a transcontinental telephone call and listened eagerly for a warm, familiar voice.

"Oh, Mom, I wish you were here," Ashley blurted out, reminding her mother of the chubby-cheeked little toddler who would always be her little girl.

"I wish you were here, too, darling. Treat yourself to a vacation, sweetheart. Close up shop and fly over. I'll send you a ticket in the morning."

A watery laugh escaped through Ashley's homesick sobs. She knew her mother would do exactly that! She was the opposite of what one would expect of a professor's wife—impulsive, free-spirited—another Auntie Mame!

"I can't, Mom. I have responsibilities here, you know."

"Oh, Ashley! You take life far too seriously. Have fun!"

"I think you're having enough for both of us," her daughter laughed. She longed to tell her mother about Sydney's sabotage, and Marc's blindness to the scheme, but somehow the mood didn't seem right. Her mother was so full of herself, ecstatic with all the sights she had seen in Europe and at the good it had done Ashley's father to have the long rest.

After Ashley hung up the phone, she sat running a hairbrush slowly through her blonde tresses. *When am I going to quit depending on my parents for emotional support?* she asked herself. She had actually resented her mother for not noticing that she needed to talk.

"Look, my girl, you can't always use someone else's shoulder to cry on," she said to the reflection in the mirror. A cold hard knot formed in her stomach as she came to grips with the fact that she was quite literally on her own. It had not been so frightening until now. There had been a shop to open, public relations calls to make, new friends to meet, and a dynamic church to attend, but now the "high" had worn off. It was lonely to stand up to the world and its problems.

She hadn't heard from Marc since she gave him the contract to study. Sydney's plans to use Ashley for her own purposes had backfired royally, and she wasn't likely to stand aside and let that happen. Maybe she had already dissuaded Marc from signing the contract.

Ashley put Mantovani on the stereo, and lay back on the couch. Tigger curled up with her, purring. Her thoughts drifted to her family again and her desire to escape from her problems right into their comforting arms. She'd had enough of Florida.

The doorbell ringing brought her back to reality. Cautiously she eased the door open, making sure the night latch was on. She recognized the man she had met at the country club dinner dance, Marc's attorney.

"Stan?" She was uncertain she remembered the name correctly.

"The same!" he grinned, waving a bottle in the air. "I brought you a little nightcap." He weaved forward.

"Oh." Ashley was taken aback. "I'm sorry. I have an early appointment. I have to go now."

Stan pushed at the door to prevent her from closing it.

"Don't be so snooty, Miss Ames. You might remember I'm a useful friend to have in your corner. I happen to know about the hassle Sydney is giving you," he said smugly. "So how about it? One little drink while I tell you what Sydney is cooking up next?" He leered at her.

"I don't *care* what Sydney is cooking up next," she said with a brave show of disinterest. "I have a business to manage and I can't do it very well and entertain evening visitors. Goodnight Stan."

His eyes blazed with fury as she forced the door closed in his face. He yelled, "You'll be sorry for this, Ashley."

Shaken, she let down the blinds, checked all the doors, then went to bed. The sooner she could put this night behind her, the better she would like it. She picked up her Bible and thumbed through looking for something—*anything*—to speak to her. The words seemed to jump right off the page. "He is a friend that sticketh closer than a brother."

"Yes, he is!" Ashley said aloud, amazed that God's Word spoke so directly to her homesickness. She began to look for another passage she vaguely remembered. "I will be your father, mother, sister, and brother." Of course, she could see it now. When God said he was sufficient to her every need, that meant he could even be her family when she needed him to be. So far he was her business partner, her protector, and now her family. He was everything! Comforted by the thought, she drifted off to sleep.

Chapter Six

June Jamboree was held on the town mall and people turned out from miles around for the gala affair. Accordian players, colorful in their early American costumes, strolled down the grassy tree-lined mall pumping out folk tunes. A crafts fair was held in crepe paper-decorated booths, the high-school band played, and balloons flew everywhere. Since Ashley's shop was right at the hub of activity, she decided to hold open house, serve punch and cookies, and dress as a pioneer woman. She was wearing a bright dirndl skirt and embroidered blouse and serving up punch to a visitor when she heard two familiar childish voices.

"There she is," Tony shouted, throwing his arms around her waist.

"Ohhhh, Ashley! You look pretty," Carmelita said shyly.

"Hello, Ashley," Marc said. Although he stood well behind the children, he spoke with his usual self-assurance. There was nothing apologetic in his manner to suggest he owed her an explanation for not responding to the Windsong contract.

"Uncle Marc said I could invite you to my birthday celebration!" Tony said proudly. "Will you come?"

"Of course." Ashley handed the children each a cup of punch. She poured one for Marc.

He said, "Tony's birthday trip to Disney World might give you the opportunity you wanted to learn their interests before you decorate their rooms." He eyed her watchfully over the rim of his cup.

She was taken by surprise. "But I thought—that is, are you going ahead with Windsong? I haven't heard anything about the contract," she reminded him tartly."

"It was signed. Sydney offered to hand deliver it."

Ashley knew better than to challenge Marc by denying the delivery.

"Perhaps she dropped it off when I wasn't here."

Ashley bent so she could have eye contact with Tony. "What is the big number?"

He held up five fingers on one band and two on the other.

"Oh ho! Magic seven!"

While she chatted with the children, Marc strolled to the display of sample books and began to leaf through them. A bulky folder fell out and fabric samples scattered everywhere. He bent to pick them up and recognition showed on his face.

"Isn't this the fabric and carpet used in the master bedroom at Windsong?" He inspected the inside of the folder and found the note scrawled by Sydney: "Use this pattern and color in the master bedroom. Do not use privacy drapes or canopy on the poster bed." Her initials were scrawled across the bottom. Marc looked grim.

"You were right after all, Ashley. It was Sydney who obviously got her choices reversed. Please accept my apologies."

Ashley was irritated that he excused Sydney so easily. Mentally she shrugged, and changed the subject to quiet her inner turmoil about Sydney's deceit. She had surrendered that to God, and she must leave it surrendered. When the time was right, she would confront Marc with the truth, but not when she felt so emotional, and not when it would jeopardize her job.

As these thoughts flew through her mind, she smiled and said, "Apology accepted, Marc."

Again, she found herself the object of his close scrutiny. He strode to the telephone, dialed a number, and then reported to Ashley that the contract would be delivered shortly. "It appears to be an oversight, so Sydney says," he said dryly.

There was a holiday spirit in the air as the four set out for Orlando. It was an odd company, Ashley decided, wondering that Sydney was not included in the plans. She and Marc still had not announced an engagement. Ashley determined to forget Sydney and enjoy the day.

The back seat was filled with chatter as Lita and Tony leafed through the colorful Disney World pamphlets. Ashley studied Marc covertly and saw he was gradually shedding the grim cloud that seemed to follow him around these days. Before too many miles were behind them, he had even joined in with the nonsensical nursery rhyme songs Ashley sang with the children.

They arrived in time to see Mickey Mouse lead off the parade through the Magic Kingdom. Marc swung Tony onto his shoulders and Ashley lifted Lita into her arms so they could better see Pluto, Donald Duck, and all the other Disney characters. Tall men on stilts and the acrobatic stunts of the storybook people brought cheers of excitement from the crowd. Vendors passed by with balloons and cotton candy, and before long they had their full share of Disney World souvenirs. Marc glanced often at his pink-cheeked companions. He seemed as interested in Ashley as in his young niece and nephew. All too soon the parade was over.

As wide-eyed as the children, Ashley dove into the fun. She was enchanted by the shrubbery formed and trimmed into the shapes of animals, gingerbread architecture, and the magnificent beds of flowers that bloomed everywhere.

"I understand a fireworks spectacular takes place

over the castle every night after dark," Marc said, looking down at Ashley.

Lita clutched his legs and was hauled into his arms. "Can we stay for it, Uncle Marc?" she wheedled, entwining her chubby arms around his neck with childlike charm, "*Please?*"

Tony seconded, insistently.

"Yes, that would be nice," Ashley added her own plea.

Marc laughed at them. "Now how could I possibly deny two such bewitching fairy princesses and a determined prince?"

After that it was a mad dash to take in every attraction the park had to offer, from boat rides down a river with cascading fountains and waterfalls to the fantasy of "It's a Small World."

Marc pointed to Big Thunder Mountain—the roller coaster ride in the Western area. "Are you game?" His warm brown eyes dared her. The children had just entered a thirty-minute Disney cartoon movie under the watchful eye of an attendant. Ashley shrank back as the mechanized monster came whipping down the steel slope in one-hundred-mile-an-hour fury. Marc's smile was taunting. "Bet you're not that brave."

She tilted her chin. "I'll take on anything you will," Ashley gritted determinedly. Before she had a chance to change her mind Marc hustled her into one of the little cars and strapped them in together. They slowly climbed the steel mountain and perched aloft its peak. Ashley gasped as she looked down over the precipice.

"I think I'm going to die," she squeaked as the car lurched and pitched downward. The world fell out from under her. A scream lodged in the back of her throat, and she clutched at Marc, grateful when he closed his arm around her protectively. She hung on to him for dear life and buried her face in his shoulder. The car slowed, and Ashley ventured a glance up. He was actually laughing!

Furious, she started to say something, but the upward climb started again and she was helpless except to hold on to him tightly—by now she could tell he was thoroughly enjoying the situation. He cuddled her close and whispered soothingly in her ear as she braced herself for the speedy descent. This time was better. She felt both safe and exhilarated being held by Marc. She loved the clean masculine smell about him and the roughness of his face against her cheek as he steadied her.

She wobbled off the roller coaster and sat on a nearby park bench. The excitement was too much. She started giggling. *Oh, please don't let me get hysterical,* she thought. Marc was watching her, and she didn't want to make a complete idiot of herself.

She sipped at the Coke he brought her and said, "I haven't done anything like that since I was a child."

His brown eyes glowed with warmth. "Are you more than that now?" he teased.

She tossed her hair over one shoulder and tipped up her nose with pretended indignation. "Of course! Haven't you noticed? I'm all grown up!" She burst into giggles again.

"Yes, I have noticed, and I like what I see."

Confused, Ashley dropped her eyes, and tried to still the butterflies in her stomach. When she looked up, his eyes locked with hers and held, until she felt every breath would leave her body.

"Let's go," he said shortly, his voice roughened with emotion.

When she stood, he pulled her close to him and put his arm around her waist. They strolled back to the theater to pick up the children. Neither spoke. It didn't seem necessary.

Eventually the golden day was closed in by the soft dark blanket of night. Exhausted, they watched the electric parade. Lita and Tony were barely staying awake to see the fireworks display soon to follow. Marc settled them on a bench and within moments they were sound asleep, propped against each other.

Marc turned laughingly to Ashley. "I guess we'll have to enjoy the magic alone." He placed his hands on her shoulders and began to knead the muscles. "Tired?" he asked softly.

"Mmmm," she answered, enjoying the relaxing motion of his hands.

Suddenly there was a stir of anticipation from the crowd. The many turreted castle was suffused in light, painting the stone battlements in pink, gray, and purple. Brightly colored pennants flew from the pinnacles, rivaled in hue by the brightly lit, stained-glass windows. A burst of light fragments shot into the air, forming an ingenious pattern of the various Disney characters. A kaleidoscope of color followed in a volley of musical explosions.

"Ohhh," Ashley breathed. "OHHHH!" she exclaimed ecstatically as each display was more brilliant than the one before it. Her eyes were dazzling with excitement. She turned to Marc. "Oh, thank you for inviting me! I never dreamed it was so marvelous!"

He looked down into her rapt expression. "Nor I," he said, his eyes not leaving her face. A shower of light sparkles exploded around the castle in a grand finale. He turned her to face him. "You look like a fairy princess enchanted by the magic of midnight."

She nodded and smiled. "Pinch me, I think I'm dreaming."

"Will this do instead?" He drew her into his arms and tilted her chin. "Every fairy princess should be kissed on the stroke of midnight."

His lips captured her own slightly parted ones, and moved to taste the delectable sweetness that he found there. He pressed her closer to him so that she felt his lean body molded against hers. Breathing raggedly, he released her, then lightly kissed her eyes open to see the stars reflected there.

"Oh, Ashley," he breathed hoarsely, pulling her to him again. She clung to him, her arms wrapped around him, caressing his strong back.

"Marc, we have to go," she whispered, sensing the crowd.

On the way back to the parking lot, crossing the expanse of water on the ferry, Ashley knew she would never be the same. But what of Marc? Her eyes sightlessly viewed the water, dappled with lights from the ferry boat. Had he felt it too, or was it for him just part of the magic of a long and perfect day? He hadn't mentioned Sydney once. Could someone in love go a whole day without thinking of the person? She knew *she* couldn't!

In his usual efficient manner, Marc bundled the group into his car and soon they were speeding back across central Florida toward home. Lita and Tony were sound asleep, curled up against each other in the back seat.

Marc sighed contentedly and stretched back against his seat. "I feel like a new man. This has been a fun day," he smiled at Ashley. "I needed a break from all the recent stress."

"A merry heart doeth good like a medicine," she quoted with a smile.

"King Solomon—Proverbs," Marc grinned.

She was continually surprised by him. "I think we all needed a break. As much as I've grown to love Windsong and the romance of the place, I have been putting in some pretty long hours."

"Romance? Windsong?" Marc grunted. "I don't tend to think of anything in connection with romance anymore."

"Not even Sydney?" Ashley asked, watching him closely.

"Especially, Sydney," Marc said tersely. "A good strong business head, perhaps," he shrugged.

Ashley held very still, shocked by his cynicism. His wounds have gone deep for him to be still invulnerable to a loving relationship. From the intensity of his kiss, she had even thought his feelings for her meant something, but she knew his interest was only physical. Tears stung her eyes and she turned her head to the blurred night landscape skimming by.

Ashley stirred slightly at a feathery touch to her eyelids.

"Wake up, princess," Marc whispered, his mouth poised over her face. She struggled from sleep. "C'mon. I'll see you inside. It's two a.m. and I don't want you to go in alone."

She rubbed the sleep from her eyes like a child and permitted him to escort her in. Her response was cool when he would have pulled her close again, and he looked at her quizzilly.

"I'm sorry, Marc. I'm sure Sydney expects your affections to be reserved for her. I think that anything further between us would be inappropriate."

He looked at her deeply. "Sydney's claims on me may not be as irrevocable as you think—but suit yourself."

Now what had he meant by that, Ashley wondered as she watched his strong erect back returning to the car.

With the schools closed for the summer, Ashley was able to hire a high-school girl to keep the shop mornings, freeing her to supervise closely the work at Windsong.

A ceramist was scheduled to arrive the last week in June to make castings of the hand-decorated tiles. Ashley suggested to Marc that this would be an educational experience for Tony and Lita.

"Good idea." I haven't been able to spend as much time as I'd like with them. During the dry weather we're having to do a lot of irrigation in the groves," he said in a preoccupied manner.

He had stopped in to purchase a birthday present for Sydney. His manner was cool, and Ashley knew it had something to do with her own rebuff the night he brought her home from Disney World.

"I'll be glad to pick them up Friday morning and take them with me to Windsong. I know you're too busy to run the shuttle," she smiled. Despite the ruffled feelings she hoped to remain his friend.

"Would you, Ashley? I have a meeting with Howis that morning. He's joining my firm soon, and I have a lot to cover with him."

"Oh, I'm so glad Howis is coming back!" Catching his amused glance she hastily explained, "It will mean so much to his mother, and, of course, I'm sure Perone Enterprises will find his services valuable."

"To say the least," Marc agreed, still appraising her reaction.

Lita and Tony squatted in the floor and watched the ceramist ply his trade. Using a spatula, he carefully spread the clay to a workable consistency, then sliced it with a wire and slammed the mass against the floor to release any air bubbles.

"Let me, let me!" shrieked Lita. She copied the artist, throwing the mixture with abandon, and Tony joined in the fun. They were deeply engrossed in the task, and didn't notice their Uncle Marc's arrival.

"What happens next?" asked Tony, always the practical one.

The ceramist had begun to form molds, using a dough roller and his fingers to deftly shape them. "From these molds, I'll make the new tiles. I'll fire and paint them at my studio in Tampa. I'll repeat the firing until we have the patina desired."

"Tampa?" Lita's ears perked up. "Sydney said Tony and me was going to a posh boarding school in Tampa."

Marc scowled. "You mean Ashley said that, don't you?"

"Nope," the children agreed at once. "That was before Ashley came. It was the time you took us to the Gasparilla parade," Lita said. " 'member? Sydney went with us. She got mad when Tony cried because he didn't want to go to a posh school. What does posh mean?"

Ashley remained silent as Marc tried to answer Lita's question.

Later they devoured a picnic lunch and then the children rested before having an afternoon swim. Marc and Ashley sat alone on the dock, dabbling their feet in the water.

Marc said, "I misjudged you, Ashley. My apologies."

"You seem to have a habit of that," Ashley reminded him cryptically. "It seems that I'm always having to prove myself. I find that a bit tedious."

"Do you now?" Marc rapped out. "Well, as a matter of fact, I find it *necessary* for women to prove their trustworthiness."

"Not all women have let you down, Marc. Just one— and that wound should have been healed a long time ago."

"What do you know about it?" he rasped.

"Very little, but there's not much one has to know about any kind of hurt. It has to be allowed to heal. Otherwise the bottled-up hurt infects the present. Dare to be vulnerable again, Marc."

He shook his head. "I can't afford to. I make clean decisions in my business as well as my personal life. I can't risk emotional involvements that could influence my business decisions. Too much rests on my shoulders."

He plucked a stem of water grass and stroked her tanned foot with it, seeming to find her wriggling toes fascinating.

"You're a good person, Ashley, but I don't believe anyone is unselfish enough to be completely trustworthy—not even you."

"Ouch!" Ashley exclaimed.

"No offense intended. It simply is true." He seemed saddened by his thought.

"Come on, Uncle Marc! We want to dive off your shoulders." He obligingly allowed himself to be used as a human springboard. After a few minutes of water play, Marc remembered the time of day, and went inside to dress again in his business suit. Ashley followed shortly with the children, unaware that Marc watched from his library every movement of her slender tanned figure, molded by the black swimsuit.

Chapter Seven

A breathless Beth Ann burst through the door of Signature Interiors. "It worked!" she beamed triumphantly. "Dave called!"

"Really?" Ashley shared her excitement.

"He's coming this weekend. He says he wants to study the blue-tails before they go into the next stage of metamorphosis." There was determination in her face. "Boy, is *he* in for a surprise. He's going to see a metamorphosis he never expected!"

"Good girl!" Ashley applauded.

They went to a large shopping mall that evening in Lakeland, an hour's drive away. A stylist snipped Beth Ann's locks into layers, swirling them forward to complement her heart-shaped face. The color was deepened and golden highlights applied to the tips—brightening the face, the hair designer explained.

Flipping around in blue jeans and sleeveless tops, the two selected a dinner dress for Beth Ann of mauve silk, which brought out the glow in her pink-cheeked fairness. Dave had planned to go sailing on Lake Lotela, so Beth Ann bought calf-length white cotton pants with a matching sailor top. Ashley found a cotton sailor's hat and perched it atop her friend's head, declaring that she would be so stunning that Dave would lose control of the rudder.

"Or just lose control, period!" Beth Ann giggled.

Ashley waggled a finger and grinned. "None of that!"

For herself she bought some new perfume and another swimsuit. Now that she had acquired a tan, green was a nice contrast.

On the day Dave was to arrive, Beth Ann panicked. "Come with us!" she insisted. "I know Howis has been wanting to take you to the Chalet Suzanne ever since he moved back home."

"As a matter of fact, that's where we're going," Ashley admitted, "but *you* are not. Howis just happened to tell me Dave made reservations at the Fisherman's Cove."

Beth Ann moaned. "I won't know a thing to say."

"Is that possible?" Ashley exclaimed in mock horror. "Then take yourself to the library and learn everything you can about marine biology."

"You mean like a crash course? I can't cram enough in to impress him with how smart I am."

"That's not the idea. You can cram enough in to ask the right questions so that he can show you how smart—*he* is! That's how it works."

Beth Ann grumped, "It just seems like an awful lot of work. Shouldn't romance just kind of happen?"

"My dear, a basic fact of life is that most of what is good in our lives happens because we *make* it happen. There's no free lunch."

Convinced, Beth Ann spent Saturday afternoon in the research section of the library preparing for her date that night.

A twilight telephone call postponed Howis and Ashley's own date to the Chalet Suzanne. Explosions had ripped through the Fort Meade phosphate plant Perone Enterprises had just acquired to manufacture their own chemical sprays and fertilizers. Luckily the personal injuries were slight, but expensive equipment had been damaged. Marc was at the plant with Howis and they would have an all-night job to investigate the explosions.

Mrs. Brody worried that neither of them would take time to eat and guessed they hadn't stopped all day for food. A willing accomplice, Ashley drove Mrs. Brody to Fort Meade with sandwiches and a thermos of hot coffee for the men.

Ashley didn't know what she had expected, but it certainly was not this city of light that stretched before her. What appeared to be tall lighted buildings were, in reality, cranes strung with thousands of lights to flood the area in daylight brightness. Dark pools of water as big as lakes, but surrounded by tall hills of loose white sand, made Ashley wonder. Mrs. Brody explained these were phosphate pits from which the ore was mined. The water table in Florida was so high that the pits filled up quickly.

There was tight security on the gate. The guard had to radio Marc for permission to give them entrance. They were escorted to one of the mine sheds where Marc and Howis were poring over some data. They straightened in surprise and walked over to the car.

"We're not going to stay long enough to interfere with your work," Mrs. Brody hastened to explain. "I just thought you might appreciate some food, and Ashley was good enough to drive me over."

"Thanks, Mom." Howis pecked her on the cheek, his hard hat putting most of his smudged face in shadow.

Marc adjusted the brim of his hard hat before leaning down to Ashley's open window. "How is the project coming along at Windsong?" he inquired guiltily, having devoted most of his time for the last three weeks to this new plant.

"Not speedily," she informed him. "There are decisions about some structural work on the roof trusses that only you can make. None of my calls to you have been returned."

"I can possibly get to it tomorrow," he said with furrowed brow. "How is ten o'clock tomorrow morning?"

"I don't keep office hours on Sunday," she pointed out.

"It doesn't have to be your office. I'll meet you somewhere else. Where will you be at ten o'clock?"

"Third pew back, left hand section, All Saints Church," she replied.

Beth Ann was late to the Sunday school class the next morning, and Ashley was annoyed. It was not like her to be anything but early. Ashley coped with the growing class of youngsters as best she could, but didn't blame the three parents who refused to leave their children in the overcrowded situation.

At last Beth Ann came flying in. She explained with a giggle that she and Dave had gone for a moonlight swim and, having gotten to bed late, she had overslept. Ashley said nothing, but knew this was out of character for her friend. After Sunday school she went on to church, but Beth Ann said she was leaving to see Dave off.

It had been a frantic morning and Ashley settled into her pew, hoping to be soothed by the quiet chords of the organ prelude. Just as Mike Gaines, the rector, took his place at the podium, someone entered the pew beside her. She turned to see Marc, resplendent in a light-gray dress suit, white shirt, and black tie. She couldn't believe he had actually come!

Marc drew his hooded brows together in a frown, leaned over and whispered, "Close your mouth. You're gawking."

Ashley snapped her lips together and whirled her head back to the front. Her heart was thumping wildly, and she was suddenly glad she had worn her new, navy blue ensemble.

He removed the hymnbook from the pew rack and offered to share with her. Marc joined in the congregational singing with a fine baritone, singing most of the lyrics without ever referring to the book. Likewise, he had no trouble leafing through to the scripture passages in Ashley's Bible.

Ashley watched him covertly. There was no doubt about it, the man was an enigma. It was difficult to keep her mind on worship with him sitting there. When they stood, his hand was at her back, supportively. When they sat, she was aware of his arm stretched along the back of the pew behind her shoulders. When she bowed her head and closed her eyes in prayer, she was keenly aware of the heady shaving lotion he was wearing.

After the service was over, he ushered her through the crowd with one hand at her elbow. Many greeted him as an old friend and welcomed him back home.

Out in the sunshine he steered her to his Porsche, parked on the back of the tree-lined parking lot. When she looked at him questioningly, he said, "We had an appointment—remember?" He steered the car toward the old part of town and parked in front of the Jacaranda Hotel, once a favorite tourist resort but now a residence hotel for retirees. Several of its occupants were reposing in rocking chairs on the veranda of the yellow-brick structure, reading the Tampa *Tribune*. Squirrels scampered through the limbs of the ancient oak trees, from whose boughs gray Spanish moss draped like feathery curls.

Instead of entering the lobby, Marc took her to another entrance at the far end of the hotel. The trellised, arched opening was aflame with a vine of orange blossoms. Marc ushered her through and she gasped with pleasure at the sight before her. Jacaranda trees formed a purple-blossomed canopy over the terrace cafe. At one end, a rock fountain sprinkled over the green and white caladiums planted in this shady spot. White wrought-iron tables and chairs gave an enchanting old world look to the place.

Marc smiled at her open-mouthed wonder. "Newcomers usually do appreciate this place. We natives tend to take for granted some of our oldest traditions and favor the fast-food lane on the expressway. I knew this was a secluded spot where we could talk, and the cuisine is still excellent."

A few minutes later the tasty brunch proved him right. Eggs Benedict served with a fresh fruit compote and steaming cups of aromatic coffee left Ashley replete.

Marc handled his fork lazily as though in no particular hurry for anything, yet Ashley had been around him enough to know he was a hustler in the work place and demanded the same from his employees. Although he had been in command at Perone Enterprises only a few short months, it was widely rumored that his reorganization had already tripled production. His packing houses were now the most efficient in the area. Yet, he was a man who knew how to relax, as he was doing now, unabashedly enjoying watching Ashley stuff herself with the delicious food.

A blush came to her cheeks as she became aware of his scrutiny and he laughed aloud. "I didn't know women did that anymore."

Her color deepened. "I didn't know it was something one had a choice about," she said pertly.

He began to speak of the service that morning, mentioning that the last time he had been there, Miss Minerva was the teacher of the boys' class.

"She still is," Ashley smiled. "She's in her seventies now, but she still relates to her boys on their level."

"She always was a wonder of wonders." Marc laughed. "As a child, I always thought of her as one of the characters *in* the Bible. I couldn't imagine even Moses being more prophetic than she was." He rubbed his knuckles gingerly, remembering. "Heaven help those who didn't have their Sunday psalm memorized, or who missed even one scripture in the sword drill. She had that ruler ready to crack down."

"Did she teach you the hymns?" Ashley was entranced at the idea of Marc as a boy in Sunday School.

"Yes, and my mother. I had an old-fashioned mother," he smiled. "For all her participation in the social clubs and her influence in the community, she was very serious about being a Christian."

"I'm glad to hear that, Marc," Ashley said softly.

He changed the subject abruptly and began to talk of matters at Windsong. Apparently he had some reservations about the expense, revealing for the first time that Windsong's future as his home would depend strictly on the ability of his company to remain competitive in the conglomerate competitions. He wasn't interested at this point in doing more than bringing it back into a saleable state.

"Do you mean you might *sell* it? I can't imagine Lita and Tony not growing up there."

"And I can't imagine Lita and Tony inheriting an unmanageable estate," he said practically. "I'm first a businessman, Ashley. Emotions have no place in the business world. The decision to retain or to sell Windsong will be strictly an economic one."

"What about Sydney?"

"What about her?" Marc said in cryptic dismissal.

Ashley knew Sydney's ambition was to become the wife in residence at Windsong. She wondered if Sydney knew Marc's adamant position on its future.

After brunch, they drove out to the estate. Marc detoured around the lake to show Ashley some of his favorite spots, as well as the expanse of the grove. Perone Enterprises maintained its own equipment in large machine shops that employed two crews full-time just for that purpose. Gigantic warehouses stored everything from tons of chemicals and fertilizer to some of the outdated furniture at Windsong.

"You might want to plunder through here some day. No doubt this is where you'll find the old wrought-iron chandeliers that are missing from the ballroom."

The Porsche took the punishment of the bumpy clay roads around the edge of the lake and on through the citrus groves. They had turned back toward the house when Marc parked and said, "Come on, I want to see if the old chapel is still standing."

One would never have known the old weather-beaten building had been a place of worship. There was no spire, nor even a cross on the door. The windows were not windows at all, but only openings shuttered tight—some had fallen, others were hanging by a hinge. The warped door groaned under Marc's weight.

Inside, Ashley gasped. The pews, the pulpit, the old oak altar, and the iron candlelabra were still in place. The roof was sagging though, and even to Ashley's cursory inspection the building was past restoring.

Marc plunged his hands in his pockets and gazed around at the place. "It's got to be torn down," he decreed. "There's no point in letting it stand here and decay."

Ashley nodded. "But don't you hate to?"

"Yes, but you can't hold onto the past. This place served its purpose. It was erected long before Avon Park had a church. Grove hands, family, and everyone connected with Windsong were *required* to attend services. The story has it that the patron of that first generation was even known to send for those who dared play hooky from church," he laughed whimsically. "When the itinerant preacher couldn't make it, the grand old man himself conducted the hymn singing, prayers and sermon!"

Ashley listened, a look of reverence on her face. "Marc, it was probably that very faithfulness to God that insured his blessings and prosperity on Windsong."

She began to prowl through the musty room which long ago had become a convenient place for cast offs. There were empty five-gallon buckets, broken tools littered about, and piles of empty burlap sacks. Exploring a large hump under one of the piles, Ashley squealed with delight at an old pump organ. It was in excellent condition due to the protection from the sacks. She struck a few chords and suggested it be removed to the mansion. Marc watched the slender woman pause tenderly in front of the pulpit as she continued her explorations. She withdrew a dusty object.

"Look, Marc." She beamed triumphantly as she held the old pulpit Bible aloft. "Now this is something from the past one *can* hold onto!"

"Yes." Marc agreed. "It never changes, does it?"

Ashley grew pensive. "I'm sure there have been other crises that other Perone patriarchs have had to overcome. I wonder how they survived?"

"All of them were astute businessmen—that's how the estate has lasted so long," Marc said. "I'm sure they would have faced any crisis just as I am doing, from a position of sound business judgment."

Ashley nodded. "I'm sure of that. But seeing this place I think their decisions were based on something more."

He looked at her curiously. "How do you mean?"

"Simply, that God gave us a good mind capable of deductive reasoning. He also gave us a heart to seek him with, that our decisions may be undergirded by faith. I think that's the underlying strength of all who lived at Windsong and managed this great empire." She turned to him. "Can you do less, Marc? Don't you owe it to your forebears as well as future Perone generations to continue that tradition of faith just as conscientiously as you apply sound business principles in your dealings?"

His eyes narrowed. At last he began to nod slowly. "I'm a smart enough businessman to know good counsel when I hear it," he said abruptly. "Maybe you're right, Ashley. I'll take that into consideration."

They left the old building, Ashley sensing that once again the place of worship had provided for the spiritual needs of a Perone.

"Windsong is only a quarter of a mile from here,"

Marc commented as he helped her back into his car. "We've come in the back way around the lake." Even as he spoke the old mansion came into view. Every time Ashley saw it, she fell in love with it all over again.

"Windsong is a survivor, Marc. It has survived its own time." She darted him an incisive glance. "Its future can be just as great."

He frowned. "We'll see."

The sagging shutters had been reattached and painted, the landscapers had cleared and trimmed the shrubbery. No longer were the hibiscus as leggy as adolescents—they stood in well-formed posture, their pink trumpet-like flowers as showy as a row of chorus girls. They made their way up the resurfaced walk to the palm court. Ashley held her hand out to enjoy the fresh spray of water from the now active marble fountains.

"Magnificent!" She smiled jubilantly. "We've done a good thing!

He laughed aloud at her exuberance. "You're something special, Ashley."

He unlocked the door from the veranda into the library, grinning as he did so. "I no longer have to beat the door down to get in my own house," he said, remembering the day they had first met. "I retrieved my keys from Sydney."

Once inside, he placed the old pulpit Bible on the mantle and picked up a family photograph album from the shelf.

The room was steamy from the mid June heat. He removed his tie and unbuttoned the three top buttons of his silk shirt revealing the thick growth of dark brown hair beneath. Ashley's pulse beat a trip-hammer rhythm.

Out of the silence they heard the mantle clock strike the hour of two. Marc became suddenly still, and Ashley could see from the flickering in his brown eyes that he was doing mental calculations.

He turned to her. "It's two o'clock."

"Yes," she replied, puzzled.

"It is Sunday afternoon." He raised an eyebrow as if to suggest this should have some significance to her. "We're in the library, I believe," he further jostled her memory.

Slowly, understanding came. He was remembering her pert reply to his advances the day they had gone to lunch at Pinecrest! He had asked if pretty blonde Sunday school teachers ever let themselves become students—in lessons in love. And she had quipped *only in the library at two o'clock on Sundays*!

She began to back away, but his forward pace kept up with her. In chagrin she discovered she was backing herself into a corner.

"Marc, be serious," she pleaded with a nervous little laugh.

"Oh, I am very serious."

"But I was only joking that day."

His face was a question mark. "Which way is it, Ashley? First you tell me to be serious, then you claim you're joking! Could it be the lady is trying to back down on her word?" His smile was teasing, but his eyes were serious. Their brown depths were smoldering, and Ashley's breath came quickly. "Marc, I'm sorry. I never meant my remark to be a casual invitation."

"I never thought you did," he said as he continued to move toward her. His voice husky with emotion as he declared, "Believe me, I could never ever take you casually."

"Good," she gasped at the look in his eyes. "Shall we get back to work?"

His smile hinted that he was not yet through with her. "After I collect on your promise," he challenged.

Suddenly she laughed. "Oh, all right!"

She stood on tiptoe and brushed his cheek lightly with her lips, then stood back, smiling at his petulant frown.

"Is that the best you can do?" he protested. "If so, we

still need to have our lesson." He drew her into his arms.

She pushed away and laughed shakily, willing herself to put distance between them. "I'm afraid this pupil isn't ready for such an experienced teacher, Marc."

Amusement gleamed in his dark eyes as he said, "Learn your lesson well, Ashley. Never throw out a challenge to me that you can't face up to." He had let her know in no uncertain terms that her inexperience was no match for his mature lovemaking.

"Shall we get to work?" she asked as she moved to the desk and picked up the family photograph album. "From these pictures I should be able to tell fairly accurately which furnishings go where."

"Yes, but I want you to inventory contents of the house first. Then we'll see what we can retrieve from the warehouse."

Still shaking inwardly from the last few minutes, Ashley forced her concentration on the family album. She became more and more engrossed as he recounted from memory the family legends. Some of the history was written in faded brown ink. There was one picture taken of a family Christmas gathering at the dinner table in the oval dining room.

"What gorgeous silver!" Ashley breathed. "I don't recall seeing it in any of the storage pantries. Is it in a vault?"

A ripple of shocked surprise caused Marc to tense. "It's always been kept under lock and key in the tall mahogany silver cabinet." He took her by the arm. "Let's go have a look."

Once in the dining room he knelt before the chest and felt with sensitive fingers for a secret lock. That released, the bottom drawer slid open evenly, revealing velvet-lined sections where the silverware should be reposing, but wasn't.

Marc picked up a small white envelope lying there. Tearing it open, he scanned the contents then nodded and smiled. "It's a note from Sophie, the Seminole who was housekeeper here until my parents died. She has the silver in safekeeping with her. She returned to the reservation when there was no longer a need for her services. She says she took the silver with her so she could keep it polished." He laughed aloud, remembering. "She always had such an obsession about the silver. Couldn't stand to see it tarnish and 'roon', as she said. He tucked the letter in his shirt pocket. "We'll have to go to the reservation some day and get it from her. I know she'll be relieved to get it off her hands."

They walked back across the ballroom floor. "Have you ever been to an Indian reservation before, Ashley?"

She shook her head slowly. "No, but from what I've heard, it's an experience of mixed emotions."

Marc's features set. "That it is," he said with an edge to his voice. "So little has been done in light of *what* could be done."

"Do they need jobs? Are they used as grove hands?"

He shook his head. "The Seminoles are good cattlemen. Some have done quite well. Others have been content to eke out a living with their Indian crafts, or what little work they can pick up here and there around Belle Glade. Some are content just to hunt and fish in the Everglades as their forefathers have done for centuries."

"Are their crafts well done?" Ashley's eyes sparkled with interest. She explained Tony wanted his room to have an Indian theme and wondered if she could get hand-woven rugs for his wall.

"Sophie can help us out there. She'll know a good source." They agreed to go the following Saturday.

Back in the library they finished leafing through the family album. Ashley suggested an archive for all the family memorabilia. Marc regarded her thoughtfully and asked for a design of what she had in mind.

He pulled down the attic stairway in the upstairs hall and inspected the rafters, following the advice of the remodeling crew. She heard tapping and pounding as he saw for himself the tensile strength of the aging wood.

Downstairs again he took the note pad from Ashley and scribbled a page of instructions, which he asked her to pass on to the crew.

She glanced at the complicated bracing system he had sketched. Her deep blue eyes widened and she looked at him with respect. This was a man of unusual intelligence. There was no end to his capabilities.

Seeing her admiration, he laughed and tousled her head. "Does it pass?"

She nodded, embarrassed that she had been so transparent.

He ordered, "Change into your swimsuit and go for a swim with me before I have heatstroke. That attic had to be two-hundred degrees at least."

She quickly changed in one of the guest bedrooms. At Marc's suggestion she kept a suit at the house and took frequent swims in the lake during the hottest part of the day when she was there to work. The air conditioning system still had to be installed.

With total disregard for feminine decorum, Ashley let out a whoop when she surfaced from a jack-knife off the dock's spring board. "How can the air be so hot and the water so cold?" she wailed.

"The lake is fed by underground springs," Marc explained, having just completed a similar dive. He was treading water beside her. He went under and she followed, delighting in the coolness.

When they came up they swam for the dock in unhurried breast strokes matching each other stroke for stroke. Marc was out of the water first and reached a hand down to help Ashley. He pulled her close and with one hand pushed back the wet strands of hair from her face. Looking up at the tenderness in his eyes, Ashley thought she had never felt such love for anyone—and he belonged to Sydney. She pulled away and stretched out on a towel under the gazebo. Quickly Marc lowered his muscular body beside her

"This is a beautiful place." Ashley surveyed the blue water edged by a white sand beach and palms. She wondered how many moonlight nights Marc and Sydney had sought privacy in this romantic spot. It must be beautiful in the tropical moonlight.

Almost as though reading her thoughts, he said, "My great-grandfather and great-grandmother were married under this gazebo. He gestured to the long dock. "She festooned the dock with the orange blossoms in bloom and candles she had dipped herself. According to legend, she turned this gazebo into nature's cathedral."

"I can well believe it. It must have been a beautiful wedding," she added dreamily.

"It was a strange wedding," Marc erupted with mirth. "The bride went to meet her groom bare-footed."

Ashley propped herself up on an elbow and peered at him. "Of course there had to be a reason for that."

"Of course. She simply did not own a pair of shoes, and he had no money to buy her a pair." He stopped and his eyes narrowed, envisioning a past of which he was not a part. "You see, the generation before had produced no heirs. A favorite nephew still in Spain was sent for to learn the citrus business and ultimately to inherit it. He left his love in Spain, heartbroken. Within a few months the Perone patriarch died, leaving the young nephew to manage a business he knew nothing about. He almost lost everything and was practically penniless. In the meantime, the love of his heart ran away from home to America, earning her passage as a cook on the ship's crew, and once landing in New Orleans, worked her way to Florida as a maid, field hand—whatever she could find to do. She arrived at Windsong, her feet bare and bleeding and blistered." He paused and looked at the delicate features of the slender girl beside him. "That's the kind of stuff the Windsong women are made of," he said with pride in his voice. "The Perone men have always chosen their women for their strength and courage rather than their softness and gentility."

A few moments of silence passed. Out of the quietness, Ashley spoke. "Marc." He looked into her eyes and saw sincerity there as she said, "There can be strength in softness. She must have been motivated by a love-softened heart to endure so much hardship and pain for the man she loved."

"Yes," he admitted, "women do have a strength bred of a different need than men." He pursed his lips determinedly. "Just the same, one cannot depend on those strengths alone. There must be a tough-minded business head at the helm when the next mistress of Windsong is chosen. It cannot be an emotional decision," he bit out.

His cold voice struck its chill through to Ashley's heart. He was making it abominably clear that their relationship was nothing more than an enjoyable encounter. Sydney's toughness remained his choice for the business of marriage. A trace of despair crossed Ashley's face. Oh, she would be careful not to let herself ever become vulnerable to him again. But she suspected that she, too, would follow a Perone barefoot—to Alaska if necessary, and if he loved her. The sooner she finished this Windsong project and removed herself from his proximity, the better off she would be.

As if her resolve were to be tested, he reached over almost apologetically and drew her hand to his lips. She jerked it away as though his touch had burned her. Anger flared in his brown eyes, and then a puzzled expression played around his mouth. However, he said nothing and began to gather up their belongings.

They made the trip back to town in silence.

Chapter Eight

On Monday evening Ashley put the finishing touches on the dinner table, fondly stroking her grandmother's Irish linen and lace cloth. Its pure white contrasted nicely with pale blue flowered china and blue candles in branched silver holders. Having decided she was long overdue in returning the Brody family's hospitality, she had planned this small dinner party more than a week ago.

From the oven she removed succulent chicken breasts in a zesty sauce made of red grapefruit and piquant spices. Homemade rolls were ready to pop in the oven and bake while she served a tray of hors d'oeuvres. A ginger ale and fruit punch cooled in the refrigerator. The doorbell rang and Ashley went to greet her guests.

With her usual sixth sense, Mrs. Brody arrived with a blue centerpiece for the table. The flowers were a wild variety, with florets clustered in large heads. Their sky-blue color blended perfectly with the china.

Talk turned to the coming weekend, the Fourth of July. Howis proposed a trek to Clearwater beach for wind sailing.

"I—I have to work," Ashley stammered, fiddling with her fork.

"Work?" everyone squawked in unison.

106

"Nobody works on the Fourth of July," Howis declared.

Ashley bit her lip. She preferred to call it work. Any other word for the time she spent with Marc was foolhardy now that she clearly understood his intentions. She explained that she would be spending her holiday on an Indian reservation helping Tony select Indian artifacts for his room.

Understanding dawned on Howis. He whistled with surprise. "So that's how it is! Now I can understand why Sydney's going to the stock car races with Stan."

"If you're thinking what I think you're thinking, you can forget it!" Ashley said emphatically. "This is strictly a business trip. Marc needs to see Sophie about some of the house contents she has stored for him."

Howis chuckled. "I knew Marc and Sydney were at odds, but I didn't understand why until now. Marc always was notorious for collecting the most beautiful women in town." There was a tinge of jealousy in his voice.

"Let me set you straight, Howis." Ashley was angered by his assumption. "Where Sydney and Marc are concerned, you can be sure that relationship will remain solidly intact."

Beth Ann seemed surprised by Ashley's vehement statement. "How can you be so sure?"

"Because Marc never passes up a good business deal," Ashley retorted shortly, scraping her chair as she rose to get dessert.

"Meow," Howis purred when she returned.

"This has gone far enough," Mrs. Brody asserted. "Marc's affairs are strictly his own."

"Right on!" Beth Ann and Howis chorused with laughter at their mother's unintended pun.

The jarring ring of the telephone interrupted further comment.

Ashley went into the living room to answer it and returned to hand an extension to Howis. "Speak of the devil," she said pithily. "It's Marc."

His staccato voice exploded from the receiver into the room. Ashley shuddered. She remembered all too well the trauma of Marc's wrath. However, Howis remained unperturbed. "I can assure you the men did a thorough job on the machinery repairs, Marc. If there are any more explosions we ought to start looking for possible sabotage."

The men talked a few minutes more and Howis hung up the phone. "We're going to make a trip over to the phosphate mines tonight. There's more trouble."

Within a very few minutes Marc was at the door to pick up Howis. At Ashley's invitation he strode into the dining room, where everyone was lingering over coffee.

"Sorry to spoil your dinner party," he said tersely. His brown eyes appraised Ashley in her white off-the-shoulder dinner dress. They lingered on her exposed shoulders, over which draped a cascade of hair from a high, twisted knot. She avoided his gaze, not sure she could hide her own turmoil. She offered him coffee, but he refused, saying the matter at the phosphate mines was urgent.

After the men left, Beth Ann helped Ashley load the dishwasher. Her mother read magazines in the living room at their insistence.

"Will Dave be coming over for the Fourth?"

"I doubt it," Beth Ann scowled. A look of pure misery clouded her face. Even her shoulders sagged.

"What is it, Beth Ann?" Ashley touched her friend's arm.

Tears trickled down, and Beth Ann shook her head. "Dave wants me to go away with him for the weekend!"

"Oh? This sounds serious. If it is, why not just make it legal?" Ashley teased. Beth Ann studied the floor.

"Dave says he doesn't make commitments until he knows a person intimately."

"Oh."

"It would kill Mom and Howis if I did something like that. I could never let them know."

Ashley said quietly, "Yes, that's true. But more important, how would *you* feel about you, Beth Ann?"

"That's just the problem. You know I can't do it, Ashley. I turned him down."

"Good girl! How did he accept your refusal?"

Beth Ann hesitated. "Not very well." She paused and said stumblingly, "He said he would give me time to get used to the idea. In fact, he implied that our future more or less depends on my being mature enough to handle an adult relationship."

"Ha!" Ashley spat out. "That's just an excuse to justify using you. Inform him that the so-called sexual revolution is over, and that a new kind of revolution has started. A woman no longer has to use her body to guarantee a life of security with a man. There are too many other options she has for living a fulfilling, rewarding life."

"Come on, Ashley. Be serious. We're all made of the same desires—to love and to be loved."

"Of course," Ashley quickly agreed, a lump coming in her throat as she thought of her own deep feelings for Marc. "But what Dave is suggesting has nothing to do with love."

"All right, all right! So it's passion we're talking about. I didn't *ask* to be made this way. Look at me, Ashley," her friend cried. "I'm almost homely. I have to decorate myself up like a Christmas tree to get a man's attention! Maybe this is the only way it's ever going to happen for me. And quite frankly, I'm beginning to wonder if Dave's way is better than no way at all!"

"You don't mean that," Ashley said quietly.

"No. I suppose I don't," Beth Ann admitted.

On impulse Ashley said, "Why don't you talk this over with Mike?"

Beth Ann looked at her aghast. "I know he's a great pastor, but I couldn't talk with him about a thing like

109

this. He's—well, he's more like a friend. Besides, he is so busy getting ready for the youth training seminars, I'd hate to add to his problems."

"I suspect that talking to him now wouldn't add to his problems nearly as much as having to bail you out of a tangled love affair later.

Beth Ann sighed unhappily. "That sounds so sordid."

They heard Mrs. Brody coming toward the kitchen. Beth Ann made a dash for the bathroom to splash cold water on her teary face.

The following Wednesday Ashley was at Windsong working in the upstairs bedroom directly over the library. She was chagrined when several cars arrived, including Marc's Porsche. He was obviously going to have a business meeting, and she hated to be on the premises at such times. It was a scorching-hot July first, all the windows were wide open, and voices carried easily.

Marc's voice vibrated with a steely quality that made Ashley shiver. She would hate to be on opposite sides from him in business dealings.

The argument grew as heated as the searing summer day.

"I tell you Marc, you're going to sell the rest of us down the river if you give up and sell out to the conglomerates."

Marc's voice came low and implacable. "Any one of you gentlemen here are welcome to buy me out. I'll make you a good price. What I'm *not* going to do is sit around and be wiped out by a setup even the feds can't seem to get a handle on. They can't even start an investigation because of the bureaucratic red tape!"

Ashley heard Stan, Marc's attorney, clear his throat and say, "I'm working on that, Marc. We have a meeting with the legal board of the Florida Citrus Commission next week."

"Meeting, meetings, meetings," one of the independent growers growled. "We've all had meetings. They never do any good. Those government boys just do a lot of double talking and buck passing. What we need is some stiff competition for the conglomerates, and Marc, we need your strength. You own more than half of all the groveland represented. We can't last if you drop out. The rest of us might as well plow our groves under and declare bankruptcy."

"You exaggerate, Frank," Marc said dryly. "Besides, I don't know just how realistic it is to say my strength will make the difference. I'm fighting a battle just to make my groves break even this year, what with this chemical poison issue and now the drought. All we need is a bad hurricane or a killing freeze to finish me off!"

The rasping voice of the eldest in the group said, "Now *you* exaggerate, Marc. I don't like to speak ill of the dead, and I was your father's closest friend for years, but the real problem in Perone Citrus Enterprises was poor management. Alicia took so much of your brother's time that he was never around long enough to mind the store. He was always traipsing off to the Bahamas, or taking his wife on some shopping trip to humor her. Your dad would never have put up with it if you had been around to take your brother's place."

There was a stunned silence before Marc replied, icicles dripping from his voice, "Let's keep this off the personal level, Jake."

Howis coughed and suggested that since they had all made it clear where they stood, perhaps they should have a cooling off period before any further discussion. His suggestion was met with unfriendly silence.

"Gentlemen, believe me, I'm not unsympathetic to your predicament." Marc's deep, low voice could be heard plainly. "If I can pull this thing through with a decent harvest, I'm willing to give Perone Citrus Enterprises another year to recover. However, as you all know, I have some very lucrative oil interests in Alaska which I can't neglect. Further, I've been out of touch

111

with the latest developments in citrus farming for a long time and I have a lot to catch up on."

"But you've hired the best, Marc," one of the men pointed out. "Howis was trained by the best. As long as his father was supervising the groves, there was no problem."

"True," Marc admitted. "And I hope Howis and I together can pull the operation together. It's only fair to tell you, though, that if we can't be profitabe, I *will* cut my losses and get out. You in the Independent Growers Association will be given first chance to bid, and I strongly suggest you begin laying whatever groundwork is necessary with the bank to cover your needs."

His voice was brittle. Ashley had no doubt that he meant every word. She suspected he had convinced the men as well, judging by the tense rumblings in the room below her.

Not wishing to hear the aftermath of the meeting, she quickly changed into her swimsuit, slipped out of the house, and headed for the dock. After a quick plunge to get wet, she spread a towel on the beach and stretched out.

She was dozing slightly when the sound of running footsteps startled her. She sat up in time to see Marc sprint the length of the dock, then spring into a dive. Moments later he surfaced and swam toward the middle of the lake.

Howis and Stan sauntered down from the house to where Ashley sat on the beach.

"Don't worry about him," Howis said, as she watched Marc anxiously, hand shading her eyes. "He's a good swimmer. He's just working off some frustration."

The two men sat on a stone bench beside Ashley. "Reckon he gave the association something to think about," Stan drawled. "Of course, *think* is all they can do. There's no way in the world Park Citrus Bank is going to loan the growers the money to buy out

Perone—not with Sydney as the head of the commercial loan department."

"Does she have that much power?" Ashley asked, surprised.

"You betcha. She doesn't hesitate to use it for her own personal ends, either," Stan said grimly. "She wants to own Windsong, and she's not about to let anyone else get their hands on it if she can help it."

"Can't the growers borrow from other sources?"

"Hardly," Howis answered her question. "Lending institutions don't usually loan money outside their local area. I would say Sydney holds the key to a lot of futures. Marc knows her. Guess he's going to have a bad time making a decision."

Ashley let a handful of loose white sand dribble through her fingers. "Well, maybe it won't come to a crisis. Maybe you and Marc can make the grove profitable."

"We're certainly going to give it our best shot. If I didn't think there was a good possibility, I wouldn't have taken the job. But it's like Marc says, so much depends on circumstances beyond our control."

Stan chuckled in a way that made Ashley feel he was enjoying Marc's discomfiture. "I'll put my money on Sydney any day. She usually gets what she wants—and she wants Windsong."

And Marc wants Sydney, Ashley finished thoughtfully.

The two men walked back to the house. Ashley watched Marc stroke his way in and pull himself onto the dock. The black swim trunks fit snugly over his trim hips. He walked toward her, the strong leg muscles contracting noticeably with his brisk steps.

He dropped down beside her, hardly winded after his long swim. Picking up the bottle of suntan lotion, he began to smooth it on her back, with a grunted explanation, "You'll burn in this early afternoon sun." His fingers wreaked havoc with her senses. He bundled her hair out of the way and stroked the lotion on her neck, massaging the cords at the nape. Ashley succumbed to the hypnotic spell of his hands.

"There!" He replaced the cap on the bottle and looked at her with an appraising eye. "That should keep the ultra-violet rays at bay."

He rolled over on his back and cushioned his head in his hands. "The coming months are going to be difficult ones, Ashley."

"You'll be equal to them."

"How do you know that?" he inquired almost scornfully.

"I don't know that. I have faith for that. You do too."

"It's going to take more than faith to get this grove back on a paying basis. It's going to take a lot of hard work and some cooperation from the weather." He sighed. "That's all part of it, I suppose—the faith to keep at the task."

In a few minutes he slept and Ashley tiptoed softly away.

Following Marc's instructions, Ashley was ready early on the Fourth. He wanted to see Sophie before the heat of the day overtook them, since there was no air conditioning at the reservation.

"You two girls look like ice cream sherbert." Marc grinned at Ashley as he helped her into the car. She and Lita were wearing almost identical pink shorts.

Lita giggled from the back seat. "We're strawberry flavor," she said with unabashed conceit.

Tony hurried them to be off so he could see the Indian "houses." They sped along the highway through the sand hills of the citrus country to low-lying swamp and boring fields of palmetto scrub.

There was nothing spectacular about the reservation. It just appeared, the palmetto huts raised precariously on stilts. A ramshackle trading post and a few other buildings dotted the side of the road. Indian crafts were displayed outside on blankets, and rugs were hung from clotheslines so their design could be seen.

"There's one!" Tony said, gesturing at a man walking along the road.

"One what?" Lita asked.

"An Indian!"

"Don't point, Tony," Marc said.

Tony hitched himself up and hung halfway over the front seat. "Can we stop now? I want to pick out a rug for my room and an Indian headdress."

"He doesn't look like an Indian to me," Lita fell back on the seat disappointed. "He's dressed just like anybody."

"Look, Lita." Ashley nodded to an Indian woman dressed in native costume. "Only the men are allowed to change their style of dress. The women have dressed the same for centuries."

In the yards of the wood frame houses, open pots gave off the smell of meat cooking for the midday meal.

Marc answered Ashley's unspoken thoughts. "It's hard to change their standard of living—they're so steeped in tradition. Like most cultures, change comes slowly—and often not at all."

Sophie was waiting in her doorway with a smile. Silver earrings dangled from her ears. She and Marc embraced as family, and chattered nonstop about times familiar to them both. Tony and Lita went exploring, giving Ashley a chance to look around. The wooden hut was better than most, though it was sparsely furnished with mostly hand-hewn furniture. In the corner was a cowhide trunk, chained and locked.

Sophie saw her glance at the trunk and promptly drew a key from around her neck. She smiled at Ashley. "You want to see the silver, yes?"

With deft, birdlike movements, the squat Indian woman released the chains and opened the oversized trunk. She lifted lumpy bundles wrapped in soft gray cloths as gently as though they were crystal instead of metal. She spoke shyly to Ashley. "I take care of this most of my life. Every month I polish so it will shine—just like the shine in the eyes of two lovers," she said coyly.

She handed each piece to an astonished Ashley, asking her to inspect if for scratches or dents. Twelve settings of sterling flatware in a baroque pattern were counted. Sophie reminisced about the gala occasions at Windsong where she had served the table and seen the heirloom silver in use. "It has life. Three mistresses have used it at Windsong. Now you will use it too. You are the right one," she said, making a quaint little presentation.

Ashley started to explain to the woman that she misunderstood, but Marc's hands on her back restrained her.

"Marriages are like fine silver," Sophie said, her black eyes snapping with interest. "Rough handling will dent and scratch. Marc, this is a fine lady, like fine silver. You must never treat her rough. Be kind and gentle."

Then she turned to Ashley. "Husbands too, are like fine silver. They must be cared for daily to bring out the polish and shine. That way, the love never gets tarnished."

It was a poignant moment, partly because of the sincerity in the old woman's ceremonious words, and partly because Ashley wished she *were* the rightful recipient. Sophie left to get a packing box for the silver, and there was an awkward silence between the two.

Finally, Marc said, "Did we just say 'I do'?"

Ashley laughed uncertainly.

"If we did, I want all the privileges that go with it," he teased.

She began hurriedly rewrapping the silver.

Marc lingered with Sophie while Ashley helped the children into the car. She caught snatches of his phrases: "you served our family with loyalty", and "you must not take on work with arthritis" and then, "monthly pension." Sophie began to weep and threw her arms around Marc's neck. He was visibly moved, and Ashley tactfully said nothing when he came back to the car.

As he drove out of the reservation, she could see why he had been anxious to get an early start. The sun's heat was pounding down, the skies brassy. There had been no rain for weeks. Even the brief stop to choose some Indian artifacts for Tony's room left them almost suffocated.

"Let's go back a different way and see a little more of the countryside," Marc suggested, pulling a Florida road map from the pocket of his car. They took the highway west, and before long saw cattle grazing on wide green pasture. Here and there a murky stream rambled through, and cows stood beneath live oaks. The road forked, and Marc's attention was caught by a billboard.

"I don't believe it!" he exclaimed with a boyish laugh. "Arcadia still has its Fourth of July parade and rodeo after all these years. I competed in the roping and riding events when I was sixteen." He shook his head wonderingly.

Tony and Lita were almost beside themselves. "Can we go, Uncle Marc? We've never been to a real live rodeo before!"

Marc turned to his companion. "How about it, Ash? Have you the time and inclination?"

"I have both," she laughed in reply. It was so good to see Marc in this lighthearted mood.

They arrived in the small cattle town and were immediately caught up in the holiday atmosphere of pennants and flags flying, popcorn vendors, and cowboy clowns peddling balloons.

Marc glanced at his watch. "It's still an hour before parade time." He threaded his way through the crowds and led them to where horses were being saddled and floats lined up in order. The band was there tuning its instruments and the fire engine stood by. Behind them there was a loud hoot and a round-up yell.

"Hey, Fireball!" a voice called out. "That you Marc?"

Marc grinned widely.

"Fireball?" Ashley mouthed disbelievingly.

He chuckled and turned to greet friends of twenty years ago.

"My Man! Is it really you?" a balding cowboy shouted as he pumped Marc's hand. The man was dressed in flamboyant Western wear, turquoise-colored and trimmed in white embroidery, with rhinestones and silver studs. A look-alike joined them, and Ashley soon learned they were the Powell brothers, attired for their rope spinning act which was a highlight of the parade.

"How about riding with us, Marc? We'll saddle up a horse for you and your lady, and the young'uns can ride on the fire engine."

Marc declined good-naturedly, pointing out that they weren't dressed for the occasion.

But "Rocky" Powell insisted on a visit. "Well, stick around and come on out to the ranch for the fish fry and barbecue after the parade. We'll have a chance to catch up on old times." When Marc hesitated, he said, "I'll bet you haven't had a wash pot full of swamp cabbage in many a year!"

"You win the bet!" Marc declared. "How can any native Floridian pass up swamp cabbage?"

Ashley held her plate over the gray lumps in the black boiling pot. Further down the food line, a speckled perch was lifted onto her plate. It had been dipped in cornmeal and fried in a large pot over an open fire. Barbecue, baked beans, corn, and slaw completed the Fourth-of-July cookout.

After the meal Tony and Lita rode ponies, some of the ranch hands strummed the guitars, and Rocky and Bo gave a private demonstration of their lariat skills, skipping in and out of twirling circles, then spiraling the ropes around their bodies until they swirled overhead.

Later, reclining beside the pool, Marc commented, "Arcadia has changed. The ranches are all still here, but I thought I remembered more of the land being in groves. I've seen a lot of open land that looks like it's going to waste."

The two brothers nodded sadly. "The big fruit juice producers came in and bought up the groves in private individuals' names. Before the grove owners caught on to what was happening, there was not enough force left to do anything about it.

The younger brother, Bo, sighed. "It's a terrible thing when people who have spent their lives in ranch work suddenly find themselves with nothing to hang on to."

Ashley noticed Marc's face had turned dark and grim.

"Hey, kids! It's about time to start back to the rodeo," she called gaily, wanting Marc to have this one day free from the pressures of decision.

It was a weary party that started home at sundown. But not too weary for Tony to mention sleepily, "I liked the bronco-riding contest best. I'm going to be a cowboy when I grow up."

"I didn't like it when they threw the baby cows down and tied them up with a rope," Lita said. Then there was silence. They were both asleep.

Marc reached for Ashley's hand in the dark. "Thank you," he said simply.

"For what?"

"Somehow, you always make things more fun." He squeezed her hand.

The following Saturday night Ashley dined with Howis at the Chalet Suzanne, a restaurant with excellent cuisine in Lake Wales. She listened intently, but try as she might, she could not get her mind off the couple dining across the room. Sydney was the usual femme fatale in a stunning gray and silver dinner dress. The voluptuous red mouth and provocative dark eyes seemed to have cast a hypnotic spell on her dinner companion—Marc.

Ashley remembered bitterly Marc's last comment to her, "You're fun to be with." *Fun yes! But who wants to be thought of as fun, when you long to be held in those strong arms!* she thought disparagingly.

"Are you listening to me?" Howis demanded.

"Of course!" Ashley said with more optimism than truth. "You said the latest explosions in the lab at the phosphate mines were caused by someone tampering with the chemical spray formula. Your lab scientists now have proof that lethal amounts of cancer causing chemicals were added illegally to the standard spray. Marc has a court case and will probably win," she smiled smugly at her accuracy.

"It will be too late to reclaim this year's harvest from the contaminated groves, but Marc can file a damage suit, and it's certain the groves will be harvestable next year."

"Good! A victory for Perone Enterprises!" Ashley wondered if that was what Sydney and Marc were celebrating at their intimate candlelight dinner for two.

She excused herself and went to the ladies' lounge to retouch her makeup. The mauve and chrome decor reminded her of a Hollywood starlet's dressing room. She sat before the huge plate-glass mirror and began to outline her lips. The lavender-rose hue complemented her dress—an original design she had purchased on sale while still in college. It was strapless, belted in tightly, and the swirl of skirt was splashed with lavender freeform patterns.

Sydney entered quietly, almost stealthily, it seemed to Ashley.

"I'm glad to see you're going out with Howis," Sydney said abruptly. "There for a while I was beginning to think you had a crush on Marc. That would be a mistake. Marc's tastes are much too sophisticated for him to be interested in an ingenue. He requires mature companionship."

Cooly, Ashley stared at Sydney's ghostly reflection in the mirror. "What Marc requires for his personal needs is of no interest to me. My sole concern is to make Windsong habitable and restore its beauty. I hope the two of you will be very happy there," she tripped over the phrase hastily, trying to mean it.

"Oh, don't worry, we will be, just as soon as I can persuade Marc, as his wife, that some things will have to be my way." She finished applying the red lipstick and tucked it into her silver evening purse.

"Good-night!" Sydney trilled in tones as silver as her outfit. She paused with her hand on the door and turned back to the young woman before the mirror. "And by the way, Ashley. People are beginning to talk about the amount of time you spend with Marc on pretense of business. Of course, knowing he is engaged to me, they think you're foolishly running after him. It would be too bad if gossip were started, now wouldn't it? I know you value your good reputation, and I'm not sure I would do anything to stop the gossips if I thought you were seriously interested in Marc." She was no longer smiling when she let the door close.

Stunned, Ashley drew the comb slowly through her hair. *What is her game?* she wondered. She sounded almost jealous—and frightened. Why else would she make threats? Ashley couldn't believe Sydney was serious. Just the same, she would have to be more careful. All of their meetings were related to the business of restoring Windsong, but neither she nor Marc could deny the chemistry between them. She turned before the mirror for a last inspection and dolefully joined Howis, wishing life could just be simple for a change.

Chapter Nine

Beth Ann squirmed uncomfortably in church on Sunday when Mike Gaines came to the pulpit, and Ashley wondered if her friend had talked with him after all. Ashley observed the pastor closely. Premature gray hair and deep lines of care made him seem older than he was. Mike was reserved by nature, a slow and patient sort. He was also a busy man, caring for his large flock, as well as his motherless children. But he always had time for everyone, and was so understanding.

Beth Ann stumbled through the liturgy, sang the hymns half-heartedly, and in general seemed unhappy. Mike glanced her way often, and Ashley could tell he had noted Beth Ann's behavior. She whispered goodbye to Ashley and slipped out of her pew just before communion was served. Ashley prayed for her friend.

After the service, she was not surprised to see Marc leaving with Tony and Lita. He had been attending regularly since the Sunday he had joined her in church, the day they found the old pulpit Bible—the day he had kissed her so intensely. Sydney was never with him, and Ashley wondered if his fiancée attended another church. She longed to run after him and say hello, but she remembered all too vividly Sydney's insinuation that people were observing them, and decided discretion was the better part of wisdom.

122

She stepped onto the sizzling sidewalk, heat waves rising from the concrete. The drought continued, and irrigation systems were being manned even on the Sabbath. Ashley knew this need for constant irrigation was another threat to the financial well-being of Perone Enterprises, because the irrigation system was outdated. Howis had advised the installation of a new one—an expensive outlay.

July lapsed into August as the heat wave continued. It seemed to Ashley that the muggy atmosphere made the whole town irritable.Customers were more disgruntled, Beth Ann was still miserable over Dave's pressure on her, and Marc was almost never available to consult about the work on Windsong—and difficult to deal with when she could reach him.

Ashley sat at the table in her workroom in the shop cutting out furniture squares to scale. Placed on graph paper they would help in planning the furniture arrangement at Windsong. Her thoughts turned to Marc, as they did often, and she remembered their last argument. Ashley had opted to work at Windsong in the evenings, throwing the windows and doors open to capture the slight breezes that blew in over the lake. When Marc discovered this, he had become extremely upset, ordering her in no uncertain terms to work in the daytime and not to be there alone after dark.

Ashley had dared to argue with him. "Now that I've gotten used to the isolation, I'm not afraid anymore. What could possibly happen in a small town like this?"

He shook her by one shoulder as if to jar her into reason. "Don't you read the papers? There were three crimes of violence last month. You're a naive child, Ashley!" he said cuttingly.

When he learned her reason for avoiding Windsong in the heat of the day he readily agreed that heatstroke was a real possibility. "Can't you get the air conditioning contractor out here to fix the system?"

"They say they're too busy with emergencies."

"Nonsense. You just have to convince them."

Angered to tears, and humiliated that he was questioning her competence again, she had retorted smartly, "I'd like to see you try it!"

He had reduced her to silence with his cold stare. To her further humiliation, he telephoned the contractor and within twenty-four hours the new system was installed and working.

·Now he was gone. He had taken Tony and Lita to Alaska for the month of August, saying he wanted them to experience the rugged beauty of its short summer.

It was an unusually quiet morning in the shop. Most of the town emptied out during "dog days" into the North Carolina mountains in search of cooler temperatures. So many of her students were gone that she had discontinued her design workshop classes until fall.

Howis continued to help her perfect her skill on water skis on weekends. Otherwise they saw little of each other, since he was working twelve-hour days, taking on Marc's responsibilities as well as his own. She knew Marc was also working long hours in his Alaska office. He had enrolled Lita and Tony in a preschool day camp that took regular excursions through the countryside, besides teaching them local crafts. Howis kept her up-to-date on their activities because he talked often by telephone with Marc.

Ashley knew only that when Marc was away, there was a cavernous void in her life. She wondered uneasily if he were acquainting the children with life in Alaska to make their adjustment easier should he move back there permanently. She had heard him speak proudly of his home there, a rustic condo on a mountainside with the most magnificent view of mountains and sea imaginable. She knew he flew his own private plane to various oil fields that were separated by the vast Alaskan tundra. Ashley marveled at his ability to slip from one role to another. He was a complex man, but she feared she was hopelessly in love with him.

Toward the end of August, Ashley received a letter from the dean of the local college asking her to participate in the Career Day program early in the fall. Ashley wondered who she had to thank for the unexpected invitation. The most prestigious business people in the state usually spoke at this occasion, and she certainly did not feel she fit in that category.

When she went to the college to discuss it, Rex Richardson, a tall man with aquiline features, greeted her graciously. He was in his late thirties and as elegant in grooming and manners as his chrome and walnut office. He explained that the annual event was meant to acquaint students with the realities of a tough competitive workplace. Ashley understood, remembering her own ill-preparedness in looking for a position.

He nodded as she discussed what she might contribute, particularly about marketing oneself. Twirling a pencil between his thumb and forefinger, he said thoughtfully, "I would like our students to integrate their careers into their lifestyles rather than sectioning off a segment themselves for the work place. Such dedication is the only way to success."

Ashley looked at him, puzzled. "I'm not certain I know what you mean. Are you saying success should outweigh all other objectives?"

Ashley saw he wasn't paying half as much attention to the subject as he was to her. She wished she had worn something other than her form-fitting black sundress with spaghetti straps. It showed off her tan well and she had succumbed to the temptation.

He glanced at his watch. "I see it's lunch time. Perhaps we could pursue this over a salad at the Palmetto Room."

Ashley did an appraisal of her own. *Why not?* He was handsome, interesting, and a very likely antidote to this madness she felt for Marc.

The Palmetto Room at the Pinecrest Country Club seemed to be the popular meeting place for business lunches. After she had selected an avocado half filled with crab-meat salad, she gave Rex her full attention. She discovered he was from her home state and even knew several people she had gone to college with.

As they ate, he briefed her on a reception that would follow the Career Day program, allowing the students to ask questions and talk individually with the speakers. He mentioned that Marc would speak also. As they finished their key lime pie, he invited her to the ballet in Lakeland on Saturday evening, which she accepted as a welcome diversion. With Marc gone, life was very dull.

A familiar figure moved toward them, undulating between the tables. "Hello there!" Sydney said, her black eyes gleaming with malicious satisfaction. "I thought you two would be good for each other," she placed a familiar hand on Rex's shoulder.

"Ashley, he did tell you that I recommended you to speak at Career Day, didn't he?" Without waiting for an answer she continued, "I serve on the committee for special activities at the college, you know, and I'm glad Rex showed the good sense to follow my suggestion. You two should get on so well!"

Ashley saw Rex's jaw tense, and his look of carefully controlled annoyance. He made some polite rejoinder, then asked Sydney to excuse them.

Ashley fairly gloated at the way he had handled Sydney. She remembered Sydney's warning and guessed this was her way of insuring that. The woman would be easy to pity, except that she was so much easier to dislike.

Lakeland was interesting, clean and beautiful with its many lakes and lack of heavy industry. The ballet, *Swan Lake*, was one of her favorites, and Rex was easy company—genuinely interested in what she thought and the goals she had set for herself.

During the weeks of August, he was a frequent companion, but he was far from the antidote she had sought. If anything, he confirmed that Ashley's love for Marc was genuine. Surely, if she had not loved Marc, she would have begun to care more for Rex, who was all any woman could desire. He was more even-tempered than Marc, not so restless and volatile. Certainly Rex had the refinement the impatient, aggressive citrus grower lacked time and patience for. Yet it was not Rex whom Ashley dreamed about.

August dragged into September, with Ashley seeing more of Rex. They were leaving a cinema as Marc and Sydney arrived for the late show. Ashley had heard he had returned the day before, but she hadn't seen him. While Rex and Sydney chatted about the merits of the Oscar award-winning movie now showing, Marc drew Ashley aside. Before she had a chance to welcome him back, he scowled and jerked his head toward Rex. "I hear you've been keeping busy for the last month. I hope not too busy to see to your responsibilities at Windsong!"

She met him head on. "I'll be happy to give you a progress report at your earliest convenience. However, under the terms of the contract, there is no cause for concern until the date of. completion has passed."

"I will monitor the work as often as I choose and take appropriate action whenever necessary!" he rapped out.

Sydney glided up and looked from one stony face to the other in amusement. "My, my," she playfully chided. "Not having words already, I hope?"

That's exactly what she hopes, thought Ashley, seeing the smug face.

Sweetly Ashley answered, "Of course not, Sydney. I was just welcoming Marc home and envying the cool month he spent in Alaska." She turned to Rex, who slipped his arm around her waist as he bid good night to the others and steered her to his Mark IV. When Ashley looked again, Marc and Sydney had disappeared into the theater.

She remembered miserably what Stan had said the night she first met Marc—anyone to whom Marc issued a check had to answer to him.

She declined Rex's invitation for a late supper. All she wanted to do was go home and cry. She had missed Marc so much and had been eagerly awaiting his return. Now he had made it very clear his only concern was how much work she had done while he was gone.

His secretary called the following Monday to set up a progress meeting. Marc's schedule was so full that he insisted on a dinner session. They would meet at Marc's suite in the hotel where he lived with Lita, Tony, and a housekeeper. She supposed Sydney would be there to approve the final plans.

Almost defiantly, Ashley chose a pale aqua dress, bare except for the spray of flat bows over one shoulder. If she was to confront Sydney, she needed its sophistication and beauty.

She parked her car on the palm-studded concrete lot beside the elegant hotel. Her silver sandals sank deep into the red carpet as she crossed the lobby to the elevator. She discovered that his apartment was the penthouse.

Her heart hammered out a triple beat as she waited for Marc to answer her knock. Why did his very presence affect her this way? She was disgusted that she had little control over her senses where this man was concerned.

Suddenly he was offering her his hand and a smile that lifted her up as though she were floating. He was stunning in cream colored slacks and buff jacket. The silk shirt was the same shade as his trousers and was open at the throat, revealing a gold circlet around his neck.

The dark brown eyes narrowed in appreciation. He placed her briefcase on the desk and led her to a table by the window set with two places and a single candle.

At her questioning look he explained that it was his housekeeper's night off.

"Actually, this was to have been Lita and Tony's big evening. They've been badgering me every day, wanting to see you." He smiled ruefully. "When I had my secretary make the plans, I forgot they had been invited to spend the weekend with a friend in Tarpon Springs. I hope you don't mind. It will be just the two of us." His eyes declared he did not mind at all. For a moment she felt caught up in swirling depths of emotion so overwhelming that she might never surface.

Taking a deep breath to control the fluttering in her chest, she said, "I missed them. Did they enjoy Alaska?"

"Immensely." Marc put a hand lightly on her bare shoulder and turned her to the window. "This is a view of the town you may not have seen before."

The hotel was located on one of the ridges so rare in the area. A quarter of a mile from town, they looked out on the red tile rooftops mingled with the conventional residential black and rust and green roofs to make a charmingly abstract pattern. Sensing her appreciation he said, "I thought the artist in you would enjoy the contrast of planes and angles against the evening landscape."

A room-service waiter brought their dinner under silver domes, lifting the covers briefly to display broccoli with cream sauce, cornish hens with wild rice, and a fresh fruit salad. Ashley shivered a little from the excitement of having an entire evening alone with Marc. She would have to be careful of the chemistry tonight. She could feel it, flowing between them in a glance, a touch, in his breath against her shoulder as he seated her at the table.

She hardly tasted the food, she was so aware of him. He told her of the rough magic that was Alaska, his second homeland. In glowing words he explained how it felt to pit his financial survival against the rugged territory, the feeling that after winning against the elements,

129

no other hurdle in life could stop you. He made it sound like an exciting adventure! There was no doubt of his love for Alaska.

His face darkened. "The only trouble is, it's no life for a woman and children—at least not the way I live up there." He paused and she wondered if he were thinking of Sydney.

"Oh, I don't know," she ventured. "It seems to me if a woman loved a man, it wouldn't be a hardship."

"That's easy to say, but the reality is quite different." He reminisced. "It's a place you can go to forget past hurts because of the demands of survival, but I doubt it would be the ideal place to nurture romance. Of course, the city where I now live is civilized and is becoming more so every day."

Was he warning that he was returning there? Would he ask Sydney to go with him?

He excused himself to refill their glasses in the kitchen, and while he was gone the phone rang. Marc called to her to answer it.

"Mr. Perone's residence."

She heard a gasp at the other end of the line, then silence.

"Hello?" Ashley said. The party hung up. Marc shrugged it off as a wrong number.

After dinner Marc rang for room service to pick up their trays, then asked Ashley for her reports. She opened her leather briefcase and began to detail what had been done so far at Windsong. Furrowing her brow, she said, "I don't understand why I haven't heard anything from the ceramist doing the tile replicas. I tried to call, but they never answer, which seems unusual for a business. There's still time before the final completion date, but I just thought it a little strange."

"Yes, we need to look into it further."

They were sitting on the sofa with her designs and sketches spread between them. He removed the papers to an end table and turned to her, cupping her face in

130

his hands and smoothing the worried creases from her brow.

"Tony and Lita weren't the only ones who missed you." He leaned over to press his lips warmly against her forehead. His fingers spread, entwining themselves in the hair at the base of her neck. He bent to touch his lips to hers. She lifted her face to accept his kiss, but at that moment the doorbell rang. He frowned.

"I'm not expecting anyone," he growled in obvious annoyance. "Don't move." He moved lithely to answer the door.

Sydney stood there, laconically propped against the doorjamb in a revealing red jumpsuit, the ultimate in loungewear.

"Hello, darling," she whispered, lightly kissing him on the lips. "I thought you'd be home since you weren't with me," she laughingly teased. She saw Ashley sitting on the sofa. "My dear, how mean of Marc to make you work such demanding hours! You really musn't let him impose on you this way," she chided.

"Can I get you something to drink, Sydney? We were just about to order coffee and dessert."

Ashley gathered up her papers and replaced them neatly in her briefcase. "Th...thank you, Marc, but I can't stay."

"That's right, Marc," Sydney confirmed. "I ran into Rex on the way up and he said he had a date later with Ashley. You shouldn't interfere with her personal life, darling." She patted him gently on the face.

"My apologies," Marc bowed mockingly to Ashley, whose flushed face he read as embarrassment at having her late date discovered, instead of anger. Furious at his quick acceptance of Sydney's lie, she left without setting him straight.

Ashley did not see Marc again until Career Day. She stood before her mirror that morning and fastened a necklace of chunky beads about her throat. The fern-green dress she wore made her tan look darker and her blonde hair brighter. She liked the effect, but confessed to herself that it was Marc she was dressing to please.

As she walked onto the platform with the other speakers the butterflies began to flutter in her stomach. It wasn't stage fright—she was excited at the prospect of seeing Marc again, disappointed he hadn't arrived yet. One by one, Rex suavely introduced the speakers, and at last it was her turn. She spoke of the training and skills required in her profession, and finished by discussing her field in relation to her lifestyle.

"I suppose the personal benefits are obvious, in that designers receive a lot of satisfaction from our applying skills to improve our environment. To me there is a direct parallel in what the Creator has done in his universe and what we do when we attempt to achieve our own Eden. From a perfect creation we draw the colors of the rainbow, sky, and sea. We're inspired by the tapestry of textures around us, and find pattern and form in the natural world. By disciplining these into a planned arrangement, we become apprentices to the master, creating our own restful, or exciting, or romantic surroundings.

"I want to emphasize, however, that beautiful rooms serve only one purpose, to provide a background for the beautiful people who inhabit them. It is the people who give life to a well-planned decor, with a warm smile, a gentle touch, a caring spirit. No hearth can provide as much warmth as a family which shelters its members from the cold world we all face from time to time. Even the drabbest room becomes a place of beauty when love exists there. A room decor can be contrived from fabric, paint, and skill, but the spirit of beauty cannot be contrived at all. It can only be developed through the Creator himself, who reflects his beauty through us."

The room had become still and quiet as Ashley finished. Then there was a burst of applause. She bowed her head in humble acknowledgement not having realized the impact of her sincerity. As she returned to her seat, she saw Marc standing in the wings. He alone was not applauding. Instead, he was looking at her with an odd mixture of respect and cynicism. Ashley despaired of trying to understand him.

Marc was last on the program. He humorously disclaimed having worthwhile advice, saying his neighbors always minded his business better than he did. Everyone laughed and he said, "As far as money management, I have very little to manage as the government does most of that for me." Sandwiched with more humor, he gave a few good pointers and sat down, leaving the students howling at his satire.

Ashley studied him unobtrusively. Hands in his pockets and relaxed, he had obviously enjoyed the spirit of camaraderie with his audience. Marc knew how to make everyone his ally.

The reception area was decorated with ferns on white pedestals flanking the refreshment table. Frosted fruits surrounded the tart strawberry punch and finger foods were in abundance. Ashley had no sooner picked up her cup, than she was surrounded by students eager to know more about her. Rex remained at her side. When at last he was forced to act as host to the departing speakers on the program, Marc sauntered over.

She complimented him on his large repertoire of anecdotes, commenting that after the long afternoon of serious speeches the students were ready for some comic relief.

Marc nodded. "Giving them a laugh or two was probably the best contribution I could make. There's really no way to teach business. A few principles can be learned in the classroom, perhaps, but as far as giving them the benefits of my experience, that's impossible. Business is something you do."

"Well, the kids loved it, and you did weave in some valuable pointers."

He looked at her intensely. Softly, he said, "No, the

kids loved you." As he saw Rex making his way back, he added dryly, "but then it seems everyone does."

He passed his hand over a lock of blonde hair that had fallen over her forehead and smoothed it back in place. The unconscious gesture was as tender as his next words. "Even I could be seduced by your charming innocence—if I thought you were really that innocent. But we both know such truth and honesty exists only in a philosopher's handbook!" His voice had turned suddenly cynical.

"No, Marc. The book I live my life by is the book of truth. It's more than a philosophy; it is a Person, and that person has the power to heal old wounds."

From the sharp look he shot her, she knew her words had hit their target. Rex motioned for her to meet some friends, and she walked away leaving Marc to stare after her thoughtfully.

The heat wave broke that evening with torrential rains beating down on the roof of her cottage. Ashley relaxed in a loose sweatshirt and jeans, listening to rain drumming on the tin roof. She welcomed the cacophony of sound, willing it to blot out the thundering echoes of Marc's words—"*Even I could be seduced by your innocence—if I thought you were really that innocent*!" How could he question her honesty, yet accept Sydney's blatant disregard for the same? Or was he still not convinced Sydney's deceit about Windsong was deliberate? It was entirely possible that she had managed to clear herself of all implication. Marc had never brought the subject up with Ashley.

"Even I could be tempted by your charms", he had said. Tonight she needed to be held in his arms close to his heart. Restless, she eased from the sofa onto the floor and began to do aerobics in rhythm with the music from the tape. As her body grew limp with exhaustion, she allowed her mind to slip into neutral. In that relaxed state a startling thought occurred to her. Although Marc continued to date Sydney, she was the only one who was still talking of marriage! Ashley locked her arms around her legs and pressed her face against her knees, considering the significance of this for a long time.

Much later, above the noise of the storm, she barely heard a tapping at the door. She leaped up and flipped on the front porch light. Then she hastily threw the door open to Marc.

He shrugged out of a hooded yellow slicker, hung it on a peg outside the door, and stepped inside. Ashley could hardly believe he was there. It was as though she had conjured him up.

He explained he was on his way home from a problem at one of the packing houses. "Can you make an impromptu trip to Tampa tomorrow?" In answer to her searching eyes, he explained, "I have to attend a hearing concerning a nuisance complaint from one of the itinerant workers. It occurred to me this would be a good time to investigate the replacement tiles. I prefer to have you along as I certainly have no experience with this sort of thing."

Ashley thought swiftly. Mrs. Brody might be persuaded to keep the shop until her assistant Judy arrived after school. Taking her assent for granted, Marc suggested they make a long day of it and have dinner at an old Spanish hotel on Davis Island, noted for its excellent authentic cuisine.

Before he left, he couldn't resist tugging at one of the pony tails tied high on each side of her head. She stood awkwardly, pointing the toes of her worn tennis shoes together, suddenly conscious of her faded jeans and sloppy sweat shirt. He laughed at her self-consciousness and dropped a kiss on the end of her pert nose. "You remind me of someone's kid sister," he teased, his eyes glinting with amusement.

She tossed her head, causing the ponytails to cartwheel, and followed him to the door. "Well, what do you expect when you come popping in at this hour—a princess? Besides, you don't look so hot yourself in that stupid slicker!"

He consoled her wounded pride with a pat on the head and left. Ashley closed the door behind him and leaned against it, overcome with remorse. He had treated her like a child! *Probably because I acted like one*, she admitted to herself.

The next morning Ashley put a black-sequined jacket in her large carryall handbag. The tailored black skirt and white silk blouse she wore were suitable for day wear, and the sequined jacket would add a little glamour when they went for dinner that evening. The v-necked jacket didn't look in the least childlike.

She was waiting when Marc called for her at the shop at ten o'clock. By noon they arrived at Port Tampa, with its century-old streets of red brick pavement. There was nothing picturesque about the heavy industry that surrounded the wharf. It was populated with banana boats from South America, barges loaded with phosphate, and fishing fleets from the Gulf.

After a delicious lunch of seafood at an unpretentious cafe, they went directly to the ceramic shop that had been commissioned to do the replacement tiles. It was open for the first day after being closed two months for repairs.

The clay artist was surprised at their request for the tiles. He scratched his grizzled gray head, thumbed through a carelessly kept file of papers and finally produced the written order. He jabbed a finger at the notation along the bottom and showed it to Marc. Peering over his shoulder, Ashley saw the word *cancel, by order of Ashley Ames, project coordinator*. Ashley gasped with surprise, her wide eyes meeting Marc's inscrutable expression.

She clamped her mouth shut. She would not humiliate herself by trying to protest her innocence. She turned on her heel and went to the car to wait.

"There's been a mistake," Marc explained to the proprietor. "We will need the tiles after all." Upon learning that the molds had been destroyed as a result of the canceled order and would have to be processed from the beginning, Marc offered to pay for the expense of the first trip to Windsong, along with additional expenses incurred.

"That won't be necessary," the proprietor said. "Miss Ames has already taken care of those charges." He turned the order sheet over. "See? This is the address I sent the bill to."

Marc's eyes narrowed as he read the address. He folded the paper and tucked it in his breast pocket. He returned to the car and brought the engine purring to life, allowing it to idle as he turned to face Ashley.

Her eyes were full of explosive sparks.

"I don't care what you think, Marcos Perone, I did not cancel the order and you can spare me any scathing remarks about scruples!"

He held up a hand to silence her. "I know you didn't cancel the order, Ashley."

She flung her arms out helplessly. "I'm sorry, Marc, but it could not have been anyone but Sydney who did that. Why would she think she could get by with it after her other manipulative tactics didn't work? Surely after you told her you saw the folder of wallpaper and fabric samples with her own initials she would know better than to try again!"

"I never confronted her about it," Marc said slowly.

Seeing her surprise, he explained, "I had to be sure, Ashley, and the only way I could be sure was to wait for something just like this." Grimly, he showed her the address on the ticket. "Sydney had him send her a bill, so naturally he had no reason to question the cancellation. She was determined to have it her way."

Ashley sighed. "Well, she certainly has thrown a monkey wrench in the project, anyway."

"I'm afraid so. The ceramist says they're weeks behind due to the closing, and he'll have to start from the beginning by casting a new mold. So be it."

Suddenly sympathetic, Ashley reached over and touched his arm. "I'm sorry, Marc. It must be a terrible disappointment Sydney was capable of this."

"Disappointment?" Marc's laugh was hollow. "Hardly. I ceased letting women have that power a long time ago. Sydney's just true to her sex."

Ashley's chin trembled. "That puts a strong indictment on the rest of us, Marc."

He made no reply as he guided the car into the traffic, expertly maneuvering through the winding narrow streets of the oldest section of the city.

Leaving a subdued Ashley in the ancient Hispanic shopping district of Ybor City, Marc went on to his appointment. Despite the incident, she was soon enthralled with the classical architecture of the buildings, a blend of stately columns, arches, and ornately carved wood. Clay colored stucco contrasted with the red tiled roofs. The street was lined with Spanish and American flags flying side by side. Ashley spent most of her time in the antique shops, seeking accent pieces to supplement the original Perone collection which had been depleted by the passing years. The afternoon was whiled away as she selected several vases, pictures, and wine carafes.

Just before it was time to meet Marc, she discovered an antique jewelry shop and purchased brightly polished sterling silver earrings and a necklace that would complement the deep-throated neckline of her evening jacket.

She met him at the appointed place, and he went with her to approve and make payment for her selections for the house. As they made the rounds, she became aware of his change in mood. When she expressed concern, he admitted the meeting had not been as simple as he had been advised it would be. Three of the workers who had sprayed the groves with the cancer-causing chemicals were filing suit. It could probably be settled out of court, but at a great cost in time and money. Marc again suspected the conglomerates were involved in inciting and supporting the itinerant workers in their claims, for few of them could afford the legal counsel for the suit.

"But haven't you proof that the chemicals you bought were tampered with? Wouldn't that relieve you of any responsibility?"

"I have proof to my own satisfaction, but I couldn't win in court, since we have no positive proof." He shrugged his shoulders. "The workers were exposed to some degree of risk, so to be fair, they are due compensation."

Back at the car he stashed their purchases in the trunk and got in beside her. "I may not be a very good dinner companion for you tonight. It has been a rough day."

"I'll take my chances," Ashley quipped.

Chapter Ten

The tropical moon ascended the blue-gray velvet sky, casting its aura on the silver-dappled bay. Silhouettes of palm trees waved their arms in the gentle September breeze as though to embrace the star-studded night. Marc stood against the balustrade at the edge of the hotel's rooftop, his arm still encircling Ashley's waist. She looked up to the misty clouds that captured the moon behind a pale veil, and wondered if she too were floating.

The evening had been perfect and full of surprises, starting with dinner. One course followed another in true Spanish tradition. Rice delicately seasoned with saffron was a delight to the palate. Chicken baked in a white wine sauce, wide flat green beans steamed only to a crispness, and a baked custard laced with caramel completed their meal on the rooftop under the open sky.

A violinist strolled among the resplendent white tables, each graced with a single coral rose.

Marc had presented her the rose as they left the table and walked along the white stone balustrade. The soft fragrance seemed to permeate the atmosphere around them.

Where they stood viewing the midnight sky, he took

the rose from her and lightly traced the outline of her lips with its velvety tip.

"Your lips rival the beauty of the most perfect bud," he murmured against her mouth as he began to drop feather-light kisses on her sensitive lower lip and the delicate corners of her mouth. Ashley moved into the circle of his arms willingly.

After a few moments, she turned and faced the bay, wonderfully aware of Marc's strong body like a solid wall behind her. She felt his arms tighten around her and trembled at the warmth of his hands.

"Isn't it beautiful?" she whispered dreamily, closing her eyes as though to lock in the beauty.

"Yes, very," he agreed, his gaze never leaving her face.

With one hand he turned her face back to his and kissed her with a completeness Ashley had not yet experienced. Pressed against him, she could feel the staccato rhythm of his heartbeat. As his lips possessed her own, she felt she might fall if it were not for his arms.

She pressed her arms against his chest. "Marc, this is madness," she breathed as his lips trailed along her throat to the pulsating hollow at its base.

His voice was gruff with emotion as he answered. "Sometimes I think you're the only sane part of my life, Ashley. We're good together."

She nodded, unable to deny the magic they felt in each other's arms, the volatile, almost frightening, emotions.

Lost in a translucent world of moonlight and mist, the distant sirens and a ship's distress wail, did not interrupt their reverie.

When at last they returned to the dining area, all of the couples were gone and only a waiter or two remained. Hand in hand they walked to the quaint old elevator that ricocheted them down to the lobby. Marc suddenly chuckled. "I haven't held hands with a girl this long since high school. If I'm not careful, I may turn into an innocent like yourself."

"I doubt that," Ashley scoffed lightly.

He laughed and guided her into the main lobby, his hand to her back. It was a glittering scene of arches, ornate gilt mirrors, and tall candelabra. It was also full of commotion, an oddity at this late hour. They began to overhear snatches of excited conversation about a freighter ramming the drawbridge as it left the bay on its way to sea. Police cars with flashing blue lights trying to handle the traffic jam on the main thoroughfare seemed to confirm this. The bridge was the only exit from the island.

"Repairs can't be made until morning," a bystander said.

"What will we do?" Ashley asked.

Marc glanced at his watch. "I'd better phone my housekeeper. Shall I ask her to see if Mrs. Brody can open the shop for you tomorrow morning?"

"Y...yes...No," Ashley stammered, unable to comprehend the sudden change of plans, "Are you sure there's no other way off the island? What do they do in emergencies?"

Marc shrugged. "There's a hospital on the island. And if anything is serious enough, there is always the Coast Guard. This doesn't happen very often—only one other time I can remember."

He left to make the call and Ashley drifted out to the courtyard with the other stranded guests. In a few minutes Marc was at her elbow.

"I got us a room for the night. It was the last one left," he announced triumphantly.

"You did what?"

"Shhh!" Marc scowled. "Do you want everyone to think I'm seducing you?"

"Well? Isn't that about what it amounts to?"

"Certainly not!" he said, affronted. "If I intended that, I'd have done it with much more finesse!"

She gaped at him, then dissolved in laughter. "You are too much. Just the same," she said with regained control, "I have no intention of sharing a room with you."

"And just what do you intend doing? The hotel doesn't allow women to run loose in the lobby all night, or more to the point," he added with thoughtful amusement, "they don't allow loose women the run of the lobby."

Her elbow found his ribs with a swift dig and his eyes widened. "I knew there was a vicious streak in you." They looked at each other helplessly, and finally he threw his hands in the air. "Look, Ashley. I didn't arrange to have the bridge whacked out of commission, you know. If you have a better solution, let's hear it."

"We could sit in the car."

"Worse," he shook his head. "The police take a dim view of that."

She glared at him.

"C'mon," he demanded, out of patience. He jerked his head toward the elevator. "I'm dead tired from meetings all afternoon, and I want to take this tie off and put my feet up. We'll figure out something."

Reluctantly she went with him, admiring in spite of herself the vintage hotel that had been restored to its original splendor. The elevator whisked them to the top floor, and Marc went along the red carpeted hallways looking for a room number to match the key. At last he inserted the key in a lock. As he pushed the door open, Ashley peered inside and gasped at what she saw.

Marc groaned. "You're not going to believe this, but I had no idea this was the bridal suite!"

Candles in branched holders cast a soft light. It reflected from the white satin coverlet turned down invitingly to reveal white satin sheets. A bottle of chilled champagne reposed in a silver bucket, and two glasses waited on a tray.

Marc laughed. "We might as well play it out." He swept her in his arms and carried her over the threshold. Seeing her look of fiery indignation, he said, "Honest, Ashley. I did not plan this. Scout's honor!" He held

143

up three fingers and made the pledge.

"If you didn't, why would they send champagne and flowers?" she sputtered, discovering the arrangement of white roses on the bedside table.

"It's probably standard equipment, automatically provided when the bridal suite is reserved. It never occurred to me that the last available room would be this," he said disgustedly.

"I'm not staying here another minute!" Ashley fumed.

"Suit yourself. I'm going in the bathroom to freshen up." He turned on his heel and strode to the louvered door.

Ashley had her thumb on the elevator button when she realized the options open to her might prove to be more embarrassing than spending the night in a chair in the room.

"Oh, heck!" she fussed and tromped back to the room.

It was locked. Marc answered her knock, bowed low, and mockingly jested that he was glad the hotel provided such lovely female companionship.

"Stop it, Marc!" she lashed out, eyes flashing.

"Sorry, Ashley," he apologized quickly. "You have to realize this is an awkward situation for us both. It's not exactly the usual end to a business day."

"I'm sorry, too, Marc," she said, and really meant it. "I'm acting as if this were your fault. We should have gone on home this afternoon as you suggested, and then we would have missed all this inconvenience."

"We would also have missed a beautiful evening," he pointed out, eyes softening as they found hers.

"It *is* beautiful, isn't it?" She smiled appreciatively, as her designer's eye noted the dusty blue carpet and mauve, Queen Anne chairs beside of the marble fireplace.

He motioned her to one of the chairs. "Have a seat and I'll demonstrate my expert technique as a masseur."

144

Somewhat doubtfully, she obeyed. At his touch, she shivered.

"Cold? I can light a fire on the grate."

She shook her head. "Why does Florida have fireplaces, anyway? I thought it was warm all year in the land of sunshine." She was babbling to keep her teeth from chattering. Marc seemed aware of it too. He stood behind her chair and began to expertly massage her shoulder muscles as he explained Florida was prone to occasional cold snaps that were fairly severe. His manner was impersonal, his hands, soothing. He went on to say such weather was a curse as well as a blessing to the citrus crop. Cold weather was needed to sweeten the fruit, but a freeze of more than two hours could annihilate a crop.

He continued to press upward on the tendons at the base of her neck. "Loosen up, Ashley," he said in a soothing voice. She began to relax under the hypnotic fingers, pillowing her head in his hands.

"Lean forward." She did so and allowed him to help her escape the snug, black-sequined jacket. He tucked a small cushion under her neck, and just as expertly, he undid the top button at the back of her blouse. She balked when he told her to remove the hem of her blouse from her waistband and unfasten the side zipper to her skirt.

He said disdainfully, "Trust me, Ashley. I don't have to lure a woman to a hotel room and seduce her against her wishes."

She blushed, "I was wondering why—"

"Why the rubdown?" he finished for her. "Because it looks like that's the only rest our muscles are going to get between now and morning. Total physical relaxation is almost as rejuvenating as a good night's sleep."

As though to punctuate his words, he began to pound her back with the edge of his hand in swift sharp blows.

"Ouch!" Ashley yelped in real pain. "What are you— a sadist?" she asked as he disregarded her protests and

145

continued to pelt her back.

"Don't worry, you'll have a chance to get even."

He came around to the front of her chair, bent and lifted her foot to his knee and removed the black pumps. Ashley had to admit it felt delicious to have his thumbs firmly massaging her tired ankles and feet. Briskly kneading her calves, Marc laughed when Ashley said dryly, "You can stop there."

To Ashley's surprise, he was right. She felt invigorated. All the soreness from walking and tension were gone.

"That's a pretty good trick," she smiled, stretching and yawning like a kitten. "Where did you learn to do that?"

"It's an old locker-room technique. In college I played football, and the only way we knew we were alive after a game was to pound the muscles around." He tossed her a towel, hitting her squarely in the face. "Now, off to the shower."

"Yes sir!" she saluted and swaggered to the shower the way she had seen athletes leave the playing field. She flung back over her shoulder, "Bet this is the first time a bridal suite has been used for a locker room."

"We can put it to more appropriate use if you like," he challenged her, closing the distance betweeen them. She made a dash, twisting out of his reach and locking the bathroom door behind her.

When she returned a few minutes later, pink-cheeked and wearing the same clothes she had taken off, she felt like a new person. Taking a brush from her purse, she stood before the mirror and brushed her hair until it gleamed, falling around her shoulders like a cape.

While she was gone, Marc had removed his shoes and tie. His shirt was loosened from his trousers, he was stretched out on the bed, relaxed, watching her.

"Now I know the secrets of your feminine mystique," he smiled.

"Oh dear, now I've forever lost hope of bewitching

146

you with my purely innocent charms," she batted her eyelashes while striking a pose of the shy maiden.

"Not a chance! Come here! Turnabout is fair play."

She walked to the bed. He took her hands and placed them on the heavy tendons at the back of the neck. "Work with circular, pressing motions, moving in to the shoulder blades...", he paused, sensing her reluctance. "You'll have to sit down on the bed," he coaxed her.

Ashley stood rooted to the spot, overcome with sudden shyness. "I...I think I could do a better job if you sat in the chair."

Eyes narrowed, he grinned. "That isn't what's bothering you. A good nurse is objective in treating her patient."

"I'm not a nurse and you are not a patient!" she snapped.

"It might be fun to pretend," he teased, gently pulling her down beside him. "You could start with my temperature."

"I don't have a thermometer," she said thickly, determined not to be drawn into his nonsense.

"I wasn't talking about taking my temperature," he said huskily. "I'm talking about giving me one."

He drew her into his arms, and sinking back against the satin coverlet, he kissed her passionately.

She struggled to free herself of his hold, but his intoxicating kiss began to take effect. Furious that her traitorous body was succumbing, she tried again to push away but found she was helpless. Slowly her arms crept up and curled around his neck. She entwined her fingers in his thick hair. The heat of desire rose within her, consuming her until she thought she would die.

She choked on a sob. "I can't handle this, Marc. You said I could trust you." Her eyes pleaded with him.

He groaned with anguish and in one swift movement thrust himself from the bed. He stood looking down at her. "Ashley, don't you know better than to believe any man who says you can trust him?" He stormed into the bathroom and slammed the door.

She heard the water running and knew he was taking a shower. She presumed it was a cold one.

She smoothed the covers on the bed, then went to sit before the dresser. She was still shaking. Everything within her longed to be held in his arms and be loved by him.

In the mirror she saw him come out of the bathroom, bare chested, and shrug into his shirt. She carefully averted her eyes from the broad torso with its covering of thick hair. He dressed, complete with tie and coat, and sat tying his shoes.

Ashley licked her lips nervously. She wanted to make him understand. "Look, Marc. You're a businessman. You know that businesses are won or lost by decisions. The same is true of my life. I have choices every day, but the decision to remain true to my convictions was made a long time ago."

He looked at her broodingly. "You don't have to explain, Ashley. We'll talk more about it tomorrow." She saw him lift his briefcase and stride purposefully to the door.

"Where are you going?"

"Probably to an all-night diner somewhere on the island. I've always got work I can do," he said wryly.

Later in bed, Ashley relived those moments in his arms. She loved him so much that she had wanted to give more. His absence left an ache so deep that she began to search her heart. Was it just her physical need that caused her separation from him to produce such loneliness? Gradually she came to grips with the real source of pain. She wanted more from the relationship, yes. But what she wanted was a true sharing between them—shared thoughts, ideas, goals. Without that, nothing else made any sense. Tears flowed freely. She didn't have that with Marc, and that was the real cause of the ache inside her.

The sun had been up an hour when a tap at the door. Not taking the time to dress, Ashley gathered the satin coverlet around her and trailed across the floor. Marc stepped just inside the door and placed a tray with two cups of coffee and a plate of Danish on the table. He stared at her dewy-eyed sleepiness and the golden halo that tumbled to her shoulders. He drew in his breath and muttered under his breath.

"Get dressed, Ashley," he said aloud, glancing at his watch. "I'll give you five minutes!" He turned on his heel and left.

She was in the bathroom when he returned. She heard him making several phone calls while he drank his coffee, but the running water muffled his conversation. Later, as she put on makeup and brushed her hair, she could hear faint snatches of his deep voice. She came out just as he ended his last call.

"Thanks, Nikos. Call me when you get back. By that time, I should have a report from my auditors. I would like to move on this before the end of the year."

What's that all about? Ashley wondered. It sounded ominous. Marc hung up and looked at her. "The bridge is operable again. We'll leave as soon as you finish breakfast."

They drove in silence, Marc preoccupied with weighty matters; Ashley preoccupied with Marc. Last night when he said, "C'mon to the room, we'll work something out later," she should have insisted on working it out then and there. If he could think of the coffee shop two hours later, he could have thought of it then!

Marc switched on the radio and began to keep time with the music. He stifled a yawn and smiled ruefully. "Last night is catching up with me." A tense silence followed, both wanting to speak, yet unable to find words.

They were traveling the causeway, and mammoth oleanders bloomed pink and white between the highway and the beach on both sides. The car slowed several times and came to a complete stop.

149

"We're hitting a lot of beach traffic," Marc mumbled, disgruntled. Here and there picnic spots dotted the sands beneath the palms. Since most of the traffic was headed for the popular Clearwater beach, the causeway beach was almost deserted. Marc pulled over to the side and parked. "Let's take a ten-minute walk. I need some fresh air."

At first they walked at a brisk pace to get the circulation going, as Marc put it, then slowed, kicking clumps of seaweed, watching the sand crabs scuttle into the water, and picking up an occasional shell or two. Marc was deeply thoughtful. When he spoke, it was with his usual forthrightness.

"Ashley, I'm responsible for what almost happened last night, and I want to apologize."

Ashley was stunned. *Marc? Apologize?* She tried to speak but he stopped her.

"There's more I want to say." He paused. "It doesn't scare me to be responsible for two large corporations, but it scares me to death to be responsible for two lives, Lita and Tony, when I've hardly been responsible for my own." He looked at her whimsically. "You've no doubt guessed that I've led a pretty free life."

"No doubt."

"After our talk in the old church at the grove that Sunday I decided to give my niece and nephew at least what had been provided for me. I began by going with them to church." He paused. "I repeated the prayer of rededication in the liturgy. I don't think I meant to be very serious, but I found that God took *me* very seriously. Those words became very personal. I was suddenly aware that I had to make a decision. I was either playing with spiritual stuff and going through the motions of religion, or I was going to make a full commitment. Well, you know me, Ashley. I've never done anything halfway in my life."

"Yes, I know, Marc. It's one of the qualities I like best about you."

He steered her around some driftwood, and they continued hand in hand down the beach. "Well, I determined right there to put Christ as the very purpose of my life. That was the beginning. One day at the end of the service when communion was served, I took the sacraments, and I heard the words from the scripture reading, 'drink ye all of it'. The word *all* stood out from the rest. It fairly loomed in front of me! Take all of it!"

He paused, awestruck. "Suddenly I felt ashamed of how I live my life. I knew that if I was going to have all I needed in my life from God, He required all of mine. I had to live according to God's Word. I knew what the Bible says. I had learned that in Sunday School—thanks to Miss Minerva," he laughed. "The important thing I want you to know, Ashley, is since that time I've lived a celibate lifestyle. It's the only way to maintain my integrity as a Christian. God didn't make one set of moral standards for women and another for men." He sighed. "Believe me, for someone like me, it's not easy. Being 'macho' is child's play by comparison."

He looked at her and his eyes grew soft and gentle. "Last night was a real test of my commitment, Ashley. You're a very desirable woman, and I wanted you more than I have ever wanted anyone in my life."

"I...I don't know what to say, Marc."

"Let me just finish saying it. I can't claim that I'm sorry we shared those moments together, but I must say that I'm grateful you were true to your personal commitments. You helped me remain true to mine."

She smiled a watery smile, wondering that he did not see the love that welled up inside her.

He bent and kissed her lightly on the lips, put his arms around her, and drew her to his side.

Chapter Eleven

Ashley was arranging the fall vignettes in her show-room. A pleasant nip in the October air reminded her of home. She missed the changing colors—probably the reason she was displaying the warm oranges, golds, and reds in the shop. She softened the strong Autumn colors with white arrangements of money plant and pampas plumes.

Workshop classes had started up again, and Ashley was glad for the extra income from tuition fees. The shop was paying its own way, but just barely. With the tuition fees she could purchase a designer line of Christmas ornaments and centerpieces. She would ask Beth Ann to help her make the final selection from the wholesale catalogs after class tonight.

The wind chimes tinkled when she opened the door and flipped the sign to read, Will Open Shortly. Her brother had mailed her winter clothing and she had to pick up the package. Ashley decided to walk the two blocks to the post office and fell into a brisk gait, inhaling deeply. Her full cinnamon skirt, which matched her softly draping overblouse, swung freely as she walked along the mall and smiled a morning greeting to those she met.

The smile disappeared when she saw Marc's black Porsche parked outside the post office. He hadn't called or stopped by since that momentous trip to Tampa and she hadn't had a legitimate reason to call him. The Windsong project was on hold while the furniture was at the upholsterer and the new tiles were being formed. Not that she hadn't thought of him a million times, hoping, praying that their walk on the beach was the beginning of something new and wonderful in their lives. For her it was.

Howis reminded her this was the busiest season for the grove industry and that Marc was preoccupied with bringing in the early orange crop. Nevertheless, it hurt to be ignored after all they had shared only two weeks ago. She jumped each time the phone rang, hoping to hear that deep resonant voice full of laughter, suggesting an exciting evening together. It never happened.

She dawdled the last few yards to give Marc a chance to complete his business and leave before she arrived. However, it was not Marc who got into the Porsche—it was Sydney. Ashley gasped. She had assumed their relationship would be past history after what Marc had discovered about Sydney. She ached with the realization that Marc was never going to love anything or anyone but business. It was all too obvious that he dare not risk a breach with Sydney. If he decided to sell Perone Enterprises, her influence in financing the other grove owners would be essential! He was too shrewd a strategist to anger Sydney! She laughed mirthlessly at her naive belief that once Marc understood Sydney's value system, he would want no part of her.

The box of clothing was huge. Ashley half carried, half dragged it down the street, regretting not bringing her car. She felt like an ant trying to carry a whole loaf of bread.

The sleek black Porsche slid to a stop at the curb. Sydney opened the door. "Get in Ashley. I'll be glad to drop you."

Ashley would have refused the ride if she didn't feel so silly carting the box down the sidewalk. Feeling like an adolescent beside the poised woman, Ashley hoisted the parcel into the back seat and sat down with what she hoped was dignity.

Too late she realized there had to be a motive behind this favor. She didn't have to wait long before Sydney got to it.

"I understand you and Marc spent quite an intimate evening marooned on Davis Island." Her eyes glittered sharply.

"You understand nothing."

"On the contrary," Sydney laughed hollowly. "Marc called Stan from your hotel room to cancel a meeting."

"That doesn't mean that Marc spent the night there or that anything happened!"

"My, we are defensive, aren't we?" Sydney said in condescending tones as she pulled up to the shop.

Ashley slammed the door. "It must be terrible to be so unsure of your fiance."

"Wrong!" Sydney spat maliciously. "It's the hired help who can't be trusted!"

Tears of anger and anguish stung as Ashley wrestled with the key in the door. At last it gave way and she headed for the back room, not bothering to change the sign on the door. She needed some time to compose herself. Dropping into the nearest chair, she buried her head in her hands.

Ashley Ames, how could you be so stupid? Instead of cooling Sydney's ire, she had ignited a fuse. When the dynamite went off, it would be Ashley whose reputation was blown to pieces.

She spent a miserable day trying to guess how Sydney would retaliate. When she wasn't brooding about that, she was mentally berating Marc for not writing Sydney out of his life. Finally she succumbed to the sobs that had lurked in the corners of her heart all day.

Oh, God, this isn't how you meant for us to live! she prayed desperately. *Please guide Marc in all his deci-*

sions—and give me the peace of a quiet spirit. Thank you. Amen.

Almost as if in immediate answer to her prayer, several visitors came in the shop. They were the first tourists to arrive for the season, and anxious to explore new shops that had opened while they were up north. Their excitement was exhilarating and Ashley forgot her pain for a while. One of the browsers commented "I think we came south just in time for a big blow. There's a hurricane building up in the gulf."

Ashley paid scant attention. Who could take that seriously when the sun was shining and the fragrant musk of fresh earth from the fresh plowed fall gardens filled the countryside?

At class that night the low-pressure area in the Gulf was the main topic of discussion. It was easy to see that these native Floridians took nothing for granted where the treacherous tropical weather was concerned. They talked of boarding up windows, getting boats out of the water and tying them down to land, laying in supplies of food, water, and kerosene lamps.

"It's kind of eerie," Ashley commented later to Beth Ann as they sat making an order from the Christmas decorations catalog.

"You can't even imagine what it's like until you see it," Beth Ann said soberly. "Not as many lives are lost now that we have adequate advance warning, but it wasn't too many years ago that people had only a few hours to make preparation. My grandparents still talk about the year back in the thirties when practically all the water blew out of Lake Okeechobee and the whole town was almost drowned. Since then they've built dikes around the lake."

Ashley had seen Okeechobee on the trip to the Indian reservation. It was large enough for ocean-going vessels. One couldn't even see across it. She shuddered and changed the subject.

A cold wind from Lake Verona blew across the mall as

they left the shop, and Ashley suddenly remembered her winter clothes in the back of Marc's car. She groaned with humiliation at the thought of having to ask him for them. And she certainly would not give Sydney the satisfaction! She clutched Beth Ann's arm.

"You have to do a favor for me. You have to get a box of clothes from the back of Marc's car for me." Her voice was pain-stricken. After Marc's silence, she simply would not call him!

"I do?" Beth Ann laughed quizzically, but then she saw the pure agony on Ashley's face and repeated soberly. "I do."

Ashley nodded. "They were left there by mistake this morning when Sydney gave me a ride. I was upset about something. I—I don't think I can explain any more than that right now."

Beth Ann promised to simply have Howis pick them up when he next was with Marc, and it was settled, to Ashley's relief.

The humidity made the chill seem much worse and Ashley was glad to arrive home. She picked up the evening paper and Tigger from her steps and went inside. A fire on the hearth seemed the perfect idea, and she also put a piano duo on the stereo before taking a bath. Afterward she brushed her hair to a silky sheen which reflected the glow from her candlelight-colored satin pajamas. She had just taken a sip of tea from a fragile blue-flowered china cup when a knock sounded at the door.

"It's me, Marc."

Ashley swung the door open and saw him standing there with her large cardboard carton. Her chin lifted a full two inches. "You needn't have bothered. I had already arranged to have them picked up."

He set the box down inside the door and shook his head in disbelief. "And to think I was actually looking foward to seeing you again," he laughed shortly.

"And I, you," she echoed his mirthless laugh, "until this morning, that is."

His eyes narrowed perceptively. "Sydney told me she ran into you this morning. She used my car to pick up some papers from the post office while I was meeting with the bank president. Her car was blocked in."

"No explanations are necessary," Ashley said icily.

"I wasn't making one. I was merely stating a fact." He rubbed his hand over his eyes warily. "Look, Ash. I have a business relationship to maintain with Sydney. There's nothing to be gained by having a major personal confrontation with her. There are other ways to handle it."

"Of course. I've always understood that business is a first priority with you,!"

"Not necessarily! At least not all the time. But right now it is. I hoped for some understanding from you, Ashley. You know the pressures I've had to deal with the last few months."

"I—I do understand, Marc," she said almost reluctantly.

The night wind whistled around the corners of the house brushing limbs of shrubbery against the window panes and sending a puff of wind down the chimney. Fall was definitely in the air. She was beseiged by melancholy. "It sounds just like home," she said with quivering chin.

He put his arm lightly around her shoulder and led her to the sofa. "Tell me about home, Ashley." His gaze probed her eyes as though he would learn everything from them.

"You never appreicate home until it's a part of the past."

"Is that what it is?"

She nodded. "The shop is my life now. My parents love me, but I think they've been planning for a long time to have a life of their own after I graduated. She sniffled and found herself more tightly enclosed in his embrace.

"Anyway, it's time for me to be on my own. I've grown to love this town and the people. You see, when I had no other place to go and no one to whom I could go, I finally came to depend on God. Signature Interiors is his provision for me." She sighed. "I could never make it financially without the free rent, and that lasts only another year. I've worked hard to build the business, but—it's not there yet."

Marc listened thoughtfully but said nothing.

"I have you to thank for giving my business a boost at the start. The Windsong account is very important to me—which reminds me. I'm ready for Lita and Tony to help select the wallpaper for their rooms. Could they come to the shop later this week, after school?"

"Of course. Just let my secretary know what day and she'll notify the school to let them walk to your shop instead of riding the bus home." He curled a strand of golden hair around his finger. "I'll pick them up at closing time and maybe we could all go to dinner."

"Perhaps," Ashley agreed vaguely. It hurt that his invitation was so casual. Three weeks and nothing from him, and then he expected her to fall in with impulsive plans, she fumed.

He bent over and kissed her forehead. "I've missed seeing you, Ashley."

"You might have called."

"I did. Several times. You were always out."

Small consolation, Ashley thought dispiritedly. As long as Sydney was in the picture—she wasn't! No way would she subject herself to the humiliation of Sydney's accusations. And no way would she solicit Marc's sympathy by relating the incident.

He turned her in his arms so that she was facing him. "Ashley, I—" his smouldering eyes reached her innermost being, and when he bent to kiss her it was all she could do to unwrap herself from his arms. She wanted his touch, but she wanted her self respect more. As long as Sydney was still in his life, there was no way she could be a part of it.

Gratefully, she heard the phone. It was Howis with a message for Marc. Ashley wondered how he knew where Marc was. She heard Marc growl something into the phone about bad timing, but she knew it had been the right time. When Marc returned she thanked him for bringing the box and walked him to the door, explaining that she had an early appointment.

He seemed about to say something, checked himself with a firm jaw and dropped a kiss lightly on her lips. "Good night, darling," he said softly. He walked briskly to the car.

Tears of confusion and frustration slid down her cheeks. She wanted more of his endearments, but she wanted more than empty words. How could she be sure, when he had not assured her?

She awoke the next morning to a leaden sky. The television screen was filled with maps of the gulf tracking the storm which was expected to reach hurricane force. When she left for work, she could sense a change. Surprisingly, it was not the squally weather she expected, but rather a sullen atmosphere that lay over the town.

There was a stir of excitement and activity when Ashley reached town. Windows were being boarded up and park benches and trash cans were being removed by the town's park department to keep them from being hurled against buildings. When the real estate broker next door finished boarding up his display window, he offered to do the same for her shop. Appreciating his kindness, she held the board for him, realizing the danger for the first time. The phone was ringing when Ashley went inside. It was Mrs. Brody urging her to leave the shop early and spend the duration of the storm with them. It was now hurtling inland faster than expected with winds over one hundred miles an hour. The edges of the storm were expected by nightfall, but that could change as the velocity intensified.

"Do people get killed in these things?" Ashley squeaked.

"Not usually, if proper precautions are taken. That's why I want you to stay with us," Mrs. Brody said soothingly.

Ashley thanked her and said she would be there by four o'clock. She then called Marc's secretary and asked her to have the school send Lita and Tony home on the bus instead of to her shop as planned.

A few minutes later she received a call from the housekeeper asking if the children were there. The school had closed early, but the children had not come home on the bus. Ashley's stomach had started to churn when the chimes at the door announced their arrival. She reassured the woman and made a fast decision. "Don't worry. I'll bring them home myself."

Lita and Tony were giggling and anxious to browse through the colorful books of wallpaper samples.

"Not today, kids. The hurricane's path heads straight through here and I'm taking you home to your Uncle Marc."

"He won't be there," Tony said. "I heard him tell the housekeeper that he would be getting ready for the hurricane at the grove. He said she could leave early because we would be with you."

Ashley frowned. She had told the housekeeper she would take them to Marc's hotel apartment. Why hadn't the woman mentioned that she was leaving early? Well, Ashley would stay with them until Marc came, and then she would go to Mrs. Brody's.

Just as she was herding the two toward the door, the phone rang. Thinking it might be some word from Marc about the children, she hurried back to answer it. It was not Marc at all. It was Fireside Upholsterers. Their delivery truck was waiting at Windsong for someone to unlock the door and sign the invoice.

"What?" Ashely cried in exasperation. "You'd deliver

on a day like this? Why wasn't I notified in advance?"

"I dun'no, Miss, but the furniture is already unloaded and the men are fixin' to leave. They said they'd wait fifteen minutes, but no more."

Ashley tore out of the shop, furious. She burned up the ten miles to Windsong, hoping she was not too late. Lita and Tony huddled in the seat beside her, not knowing what to think of her angry state.

By the time they were halfway there, the winds were gusting. When she turned onto the grove road, she was surprised to see the amount of fruit on the ground just from the high winds. She knew this was a crucial time for the citrus industry, and for Perone Enterprises in particular. She was heartsick to see the carefully nurtured crop lying on the ground!

A gale blew her small Escort to the side of the road and the children screamed. "It's O.K.," Ashley comforted them. "I'm just going to be a minute here, and then I'll take you to your Uncle Marc." She breathed a sigh of relief as the wind died down a bit.

With instruction to the children to wait in the car, Ashley directed the delivery men where to place the furniture, inspecting each piece as they brought it in. Finally she signed the receipt, after refusing a pair of chairs that had been covered with the wrong fabric. Quite a few minutes had passed before she locked the house and returned to the car.

"Where's Tony?" she asked Lita.

The child pointed a chubby finger toward the lake. "He went to get his ducky raft."

"Oh, no!" Ashley wailed. "Wait here!" She ran to the back of the house to get him. She was just in time to see a gust of wind blow the toy out of Tony's reach toward the grove. He chased it.

"Tony! Come back!" she ordered.

"In a minute! I don't want ducky to get losted."

"Now!" Ashley yelled, following him. She lost sight of him, but saw the toy raft sail over a treetop. Knowing

Tony would be in hot pursuit, she ran to catch up with him. "Tony! Come back! We have to leave. The storm is almost here!" The words blew back into her throat as a gust of wind blasted her in the face and blew her slender form backward. Swirling sand blotted out any sight of the child.

"Tony! If you can hear me, answer!" Even the wind was silent. Real anxiety began to churn her stomach. Up until now, she had taken it for granted that she would beat the storm and deliver the children safe and sound, but she hadn't counted on the storm advancing this rapidly.

"Ashley! Wait for me."

Ashley wheeled and saw Lita following her, crying because sand was in her eyes. Ashley hurried back and swooped the child into her arms. "Why didn't you wait as I told you?"

Lita began to cry. "Cause I'm scared," she wailed.

"We've got to find Tony," Ashley said, plunging deeper into the grove. The wind blew her hair into her eyes, and the stinging sand made progress almost impossible.

"Tony! Tony!" she called continually, trying to keep the panic out of her voice for Lita's sake.

The deep, loose sand was heavy under her feet as she pressed on through the rows of trees, each just like the other. She braced herself against the onslaught of another gale. It was so swift it blew the breath right back into her body, making it momentarily impossible to breathe. There was a snapping sound, and a large tree branch blew to the ground beside her just two feet away. She remembered T.V. warnings that said flying debris was one of the greatest dangers of a hurricane.

After the gale slackened, Lita suddenly wiggled in Ashley's arms and pointed a chubby finger. "There he is." Under the low branches of an orange tree sat Tony, duck raft firmly clenched in his arms.

"Come here this minute!" Ashley yelled, creating a

furor of her own. The frightened boy was all too glad to grab onto Ashley's arm as she tried to make her way from the grove. She stopped to get her bearings. They had long since lost sight of Windsong and the lake. She had no idea how far they had come. It suddenly occurred to her that it was much too early for the darkness that had settled in. Almost simultaneously with her thought, the clouds opened up and a torrent descended. The children clung to her.

"I'm afraid!" Tony said solemnly.

Ashley would have laughed at his expression, except that a roll of thunder blotted out anything funny. A crack of lightning lit up the sky, and Ashley saw the tree limbs thrashing wildly. Thinking to herself that they might wander around in the grove all night, she wondered if Tony's solution was the best. Perhaps they would just get under a tree for whatever protection they could find. No! She remembered that was not the thing to do.

She was struck with terror. After a week of warnings on radio and T.V., she had still managed to get herself caught out in the storm. Marc would be furious! She began to pray for direction. Only the thunder and lightning answered, or so it seemed.

In the distance, against a lightning-whited sky, Ashley saw the old church silhouetted. A shelter!

She hurried the children forward, and they reached it before the next fury of the wind was unleashed. It was a poor shelter, for the pummeling winds rattled the old timbers with unbelievable viciousness. Lita whimpered and refused to be put down. Tony begged to be picked up. Despairingly, Ashley knew she had to do something to quell their fears. She remembered the old pump organ and lost no time uncovering it. In the eerie light of the storm she showed them how to pump the bellows while she picked out a tune.

The shutters had blown open, and there was nothing to protect the interior from the elements, the glass windows having long since disappeared. The winds howled past the gaping openings, but mercifully the rain was slight between squalls. Gray light filled the place, but Ashley knew it wouldn't be long before night would bring total darkness. It must be at least five o'clock by now.

The storm hit in earnest. The children grew restless and fearful. Lita tugged at her hand. "I wanna go home, Ashley. I want Uncle Marc."

Tony patted his sister's head. "It's all right. 'Member, Ashley taught us in Sunday School that God stopped the storm when the disciples were about to shipwreck? Maybe God will stop this storm too."

Lita looked up at her trustingly. "Is that right, Ashley?"

Ashley put her arms around them both as they sat beside her at the organ. She wanted to weep. How could she answer? It was one thing to talk about Jesus stilling the storm on a sunny Sunday two thousand years after it happened, but what about now, in the midst of it? Praying for wisdom, she answered, "Yes, Jesus calms the storm, but sometimes he allows us to go through it, and gives us a calm spirit so we're not afraid, as He is with us."

Then she remembered the words engraved on the old hearthstone at Windsong. Mustering a smile, she began to finger the notes of the organ, making up a tune as she went. She sang the words to the children:

A Mighty Man of valor doth ride upon the wind.
His mercy is upon us as stormy blasts descend.
But then a song of comfort comes singing through the trees:
God is our calm in trouble, our wind song in storm's breeze.

Lita clapped her hands. "I want to sing it too!"
They made a game of it, vying to see which of them

164

could sing louder than the wind, which was now lashing in fury. The door crashed open and the trio screamed in astonishment. Marc rushed in. Only then did Ashley see the headlights to the jeep streaming through the darkness.

They rushed to meet him, and like a cracking whip he ordered them into the jeep, making the children and Ashley crouch in the floorboards. He threw burlap sacks and what other protection he could find over their backs. Then began the journey against the wind.

Mercifully, there was a lull in the storm, allowing Marc to cover the short distance to Windsong without mishap. As he braked under the portico, the winds rose again, and Ashley was startled to see five foot waves on Lake Lotela.

They lost no time dashing into the house, Lita and Tony racing to look through the cracks in the boarded-up windows, still not fully understanding the danger they were in.

But Ashley fell into Marc's arms on a wave of aftershock. She shook with sobs so that she hardly comprehended the words torn from his very soul.

"Ashley, oh Ashley!" He gripped her tightly and began rocking back and forth. Hoarse with emotion, he said, "How could I bear it if anything had happened to you? My life would be worth nothing!" He buried his head in the soft curve of her neck and whispered, "My beautiful, darling Ashley."

She wrapped her arms around his neck. "H—how did you know where to find us?" she asked when she found her breath.

"When I brought the crews to board up the windows, I saw your car, and guessed that you had gone into the grove for heaven only knows what reason.

"Tony's ducky raft," Ashley interjected dryly.

"I left the men to finish the windows, took the jeep and started looking for you. I had just about given up hope," his voice caught, "then I heard the music." He looked at her tenderly, and his hands gently cupped her face. "It was the wind song, Ashley. I heard you singing the wind song, and I knew you were at the church." He held her close to his heart and she met his lips eagerly.

"Hey, you two. I'm hungry." Tony announced.

They broke apart to include Tony and Lita in their embrace, and Ashley said, "I had some groceries in the car." Marc went to get the sack while Ashley called Mrs. Brody before the phone lines went down.

The winds seemed much less fierce from the shelter of the house than they had in the old church. Marc informed her she had only seen the squalls and gales that preceded a hurricane. "I would never have gotten two feet beyond the door if I had tried to find you in the full force of the winds."

While they still had electricity, Ashley made pancakes on the griddle of the new stove, pouring them into animal caricature shapes to distract the children. She cooked link sausages and warmed the maple syrup, then she made coffee for herself and Marc in the percolator which she kept there for use when she was working. She was using the groceries Mrs. Brody had asked her to pick up on her way out. *What a twist of fate,* Ashley thought.

As predicted, the lights went off and they found themselves eating by firelight in the large living room.

"Well, we're dining together according to plan, even if the circumstances are different," Marc smiled, reminding Ashley of his invitation several nights ago.

"You generally do get your way," she said tersely. She found herself a little shy of him, now that he had spoken so fervently to her. There was a delicious tickling in her heart at the anticipation of more to come.

They listened to the fiercely driving wind and the cracking of branches as trees whipped loose their limbs. Marc roved aimlessly about, checking the windows and doors, and reading the barometer.

Ashley asked the children to clean up the plastic

plates and forks they had eaten from, and went to join him. She slipped her hand in his.

"Listen to that wind. It's blowing money right off the trees!"

Hearing him talk, Ashley knew this could very well be the end of Perone Enterprises. Marc had done everything humanly possible, but she knew from the grimness of his face that this might be the last straw.

"We have to believe that it will come out right, Marc. Win, lose, succeed, fail, or draw, we are the Lord's."

"That's true, Ashley."

As the night wore on, the air grew cold, and the four curled up under blankets in front of the fire. Marc periodically made his rounds to check the house, listening to the battery-operated weather radio. The children slept from the exhaustion of the excitement.

Now and then Marc glanced her way from his chair when he thought she was dozing on the sofa. Once she smiled and he returned it. He was about to speak, then he seemed to rethink his words and said nothing.

At the height of the hurricane, wind blasts hit the sides of the house like sledge hammers. Ashley trembled. Marc came to sit beside her on the sofa, making his presence a comfort. But he didn't touch her. It was as though he purposely restrained himself. Ashley longed for his touch, and for some endearment. He said nothing, and she wondered if she had imagined his impassioned need of her.

Chapter Twelve

The last of the cleanup crews were leaving when Ashley arrived at Windsong several days later. She had been unable to believe the devastation the storm had wrought in Avon Park, but now she was unable to believe the rapidity with which the town was restored to order. Damage to the citrus crop had been heavy, and fruit lying thick under the trees remained the most visible part of the storm damage.

She was meeting a seamstress at Windsong to take measurements for custom-made draperies in the ballroom area. She was dismayed to see a number of cars parked in the drive and realized that a business meeting was in progress. Intense voices sounded from the library doorway as Marc walked out, deep in conversation with another man. Both men were laughing, and when Howis and Stan joined them, they were just as cheerful. No one could ever guess they had just lost a half million dollars worth of fruit.

Ashley slipped inside and perched on a stepladder to measure the transom over the front door. The men were talking on the veranda. She heard the man Marc called Nikos assure him that he expected to liquidate the Perone real estate holdings in thirty days and close the offices in two months. Marc seemed delighted.

Ashley was paralyzed. Marc was throwing in the

towel on Perone Enterprises! Her head began to reel. What would happen to Windsong? And why had Howis seemed so pleased? Of course, Marc was offering him a better position in his Alaskan oil company. That would be like him.

It was mid-afternoon when she and the seamstress finished taking measurements. Ashley's head ached as she prepared to leave. But just then a car arrived, and several women of varying ages made their way to the door. Ashley knew a committee when she saw one, but had no earthly idea what they were about.

"Mr. Perone said we would find you here and that you would be glad to show us around the premises," a stout woman said, after introducing herself as the chairwoman of the local historical society. "We're so excited at the prospect of having Windsong."

Mesmerized by this second shock, Ashley led the way through the house. How could Marc let go of the family estate with so little effort? He might at least have said something to her. She was furious with him and with herself. How could she have thought his words of love meant anything? They were as worthless as the lost moments it took to say them. Of course, he had found the ideal solution. Donating Windsong to the historical society was a stroke of genius. Not only would it be preserved as part of the region's history, but he would get a hefty tax write-off. Oh, yes! He was a shrewd businessman!

After an agonizing hour of hostessing the tour, Ashley saw the visitors off and slumped in a chair for a good cry. How dare Marc presume upon her this way without advance warning of the visitors? In her heart, she knew that wasn't the real hurt. The real hurt was that he had let Windsong go at all. She loved it and she loved its owner. She wanted nothing more than to have them both.

At noon the next day, Marc called. "I'm on my way to the airport, Ashley. I'll be in Alaska for a month." His tones were business-like. "According to the terms of the Windsong contract you're past the finish date for completing the project. I would like to get this matter settled before I leave."

"I'm aware of that," Ashley answered in tones just as incisive. "I think you are also aware there have been several delays that were not my doing."

"I understand perfectly. What I'm asking is for you to finish no later than thirty days from now. Do you see any problem with that?"

"Of course not! I can complete it in two weeks if you wish!" Anger crackled in her voice. Marc had never indicated that time was a problem. Now suddenly, he was demanding a finish date.

"Thirty days will be fine." There was an infuriating hint of amusement in his voice.

"Is that all? A customer has just come into the shop." Even to herself she sounded belligerent.

"Not quite," he said smoothly. There was a long pause as he seemed to carefully choose his words. "There's a lot I wanted to explain to you before I leave, but things have piled up here in the office, and I have a plane to catch. Some of it I could say on the phone, but since you have a customer I won't take your time. There'll be time to talk when I get back from Alaska."

No explanations necessary, Marc, she thought bitterly. *I've already found out the hard way what you had to tell me*!

Ashley went right to work on Windsong the next day. She had other reasons to hurry besides Marc's sharp rebuke. Now that she knew the future of Windsong, it wrenched her heart to go there. It hurt to realize that never again would its rooms resound with the happy laughter of children or the tender love words spoken between man and wife. It was doomed to become a hollow shell of the past. The ache was so great, she wanted to complete her duties at the mansion as speedily as possible.

There was another reason as well. Her brother Brad's wife had discovered his business loan to her, and there was trouble! On the phone, they had both been kind and courteous to her, but she knew them well enough to sense something was drastically wrong. As soon as the Windsong account was complete she could collect her fee and pay most of the money back.

The painting and papering were almost done. Ashley stayed on hand most of the time to make sure the wallpaper and paint colors ended up in the right rooms. She returned to the shop late one afternoon, tired, paint-smeared, and burned out from the grueling pace, to find a registered letter awaiting her. Bemused, she tore it open. For long moments she sat, disbelieving and unseeing. How could Marc have done this? He knew she could not survive as a business except for the free rent of the shop. She read the cold, official words again.

"Due to reorganization of Perone Enterprises and reallocation of assets, we are liquidating all real estate holdings, which includes the premises of Signature Interiors. This letter is official notification that the premises must be vacated within thirty days."

The letter went on to express regrets and offer assistance in relocation. Ashley hadn't even realized the block of buildings belonged to Perone Enterprises. According to further details, they had been leased to the Urban Renewal Project for one dollar a year and tax benefits.

Relocation? It was out of the question. She couldn't afford to rent a chicken coop. She read the letter again and again to be sure she had absorbed every detail. It was signed by Stan Wittmore, the company attorney. She called his office to see if she could have an extension, a little more time to negotiate a loan and purchase her store. Stan reported that the block of buildings had already been sold.

"In fact," he said, and she thought he sounded a little embarrassed, "the new owner of the building would

171

like to purchase your inventory if you don't plan to relocate." She was speechless. The whole thing had become a nightmare. Not only had Marc walked out of her life with scarcely a farewell, he had handed over her beloved Windsong to strangers, and now had dealt a death blow to her business as well! The man she loved had betrayed her in every way.

And now nothing else mattered. Bitterly, she agreed to take inventory and have a figure ready for him by the end of the week. At least Brad would not be the loser in all this. When she was paid for the inventory, she would be able to repay the full amount of his loan, with enough left over to live on until she could find a job. She now had experience to offer. It was scant compensation.

On her knees beside her bed that night Ashley's prayer was tearful. She remembered painfully the confidence she had shared with Marc that Siqnature Interiors was a provision of the Lord. Now Marc was flinging that back in her face—because nothing mattered to him but his own business.

Ashley worked two days at Windsong to get the drapes hung after the painters and wallpaper hangers were finished. She worked late in the evenings hanging pictures and placing accessories. She was driven by the need to leave Avon Park before Marc returned. There was a limit to the trauma she could stand, and she knew she couldn't handle seeing him again. Her life had fallen apart, but she didn't have to expose her hurt to the one who had inflicted it.

All was in place at Windsong, except the handmade tiles, which were still being fired. The drapes were hung and only unfinished cornices and tiebacks remained to be added. The upholsterer would deliver the two chairs, redone in the correct fabric, next week—but she would be gone by then. Her work with Windsong was finished.

On her last day at the lake cottage Ashley packed her

bags and took care of winterizing the cottage. She still had a few hours before the farewell dinner Mrs. Brody had planned. At Ashley's request it would just be Beth Ann, Mrs. Brody and herself. Since it was not an occasion for celebration, Ashley could not bear to be around anyone other than those closest to her. Howis was in Alaska with Marc—looking over his new position, she supposed. She regretted not seeing him before she left. He had been a true friend.

She had cleared her desk yesterday at the shop, refusing to cry, forcing herself to admit that it was only mortar and brick, fabric and art fantasies—hardly the materials of which life was made.

But Windsong was a different matter. In the hours remaining, she made one last trip out there. Despite the wounds in her spirit, she could still find room for gratitude. Whatever else had happened, God had truly been generous to allow her the pleasure of restoring this mansion to its splendor.

She went from room to room, lovingly stroking the mellowed patina of the antique pieces, feasting one last time on the beauty of the arched windows, and saying farewell to the family portraits in the green-silk, oval dining room. How could she let it go? Tears filled her eyes.

A quiet voice seemed to say, "But it's not yours Ashley. It's mine." It was then she realized she had emotionally taken ownership of Windsong and that all of our possessions in this life are temporary. With that realization she was able to surrender it at last.

"I still don't understand all that has happened," Mrs. Brody said at dinner, shaking her head sadly. "I know Marc would not intentionally hurt you by selling the building."

"I don't think it was necessarily intentional. Marc had a business decision to make, and just like all good businessmen, he made it!" Ashley was determined to be objective.

Beth Ann objected, and her mother shook her head again. "Howis hasn't mentioned a word about this. In fact, he has been unusually close-mouthed about Perone Enterprises lately. I knew there was a transition going on, but he never said there would be any drastic changes."

Ashley's hand was unsteady as she lifted her glass of iced tea. "There's an old saying in business, Mrs. Brody," she laughed shakily, "Loose lips sink ships. I'm sure Marc's employees knew their jobs were on the line if any news had leaked before he was ready for a news release."

The meal was delicious and beautifully served, but Ashley could only taste bittersweetness as their time together drew to a close. "It's my last night here and I don't want to spend it alone. Come spend the night, Beth Ann, please?"

"Of course," Beth Ann nodded. "We'll have one last heart-to-heart before you go." She smiled, gulping back the tears.

"Not too late," Mrs. Brody cautioned. "Ashley plans an early morning start."

At the door Ashley laid her head on Mrs. Brody's shoulder and thanked her for all she had meant in her life. Mrs. Brody lifted the young woman's face, childlike in its hurt, and said, "Ashley, you must believe that whatever happens is right for you. Win or lose, succeed or fail, you are the Lord's."

Ashley burst into tears at the familiar quotation, remembering when she and Marc had come to that same understanding. She sobbed heartbreakingly. "Marc has won. I've lost. He has everything he wanted, and I've lost everything that had meaning in my life."

"Perhaps it seems that way now. Forgive Marc for whatever you think he has done. That will make you the winner, ultimately."

The words rang in her ears as she and Beth Ann walked down the street to Ashley's cottage. *Forgive him? Impossible!* She might not be able to stop her heart from loving him, but she could never forgive him!

The flames leaped on the cottage hearth in a contemporary dance, cracking and snapping. Beth Ann and Ashley had decided they could use a manicure and were sprawled on the floor beside the coffee table which held an assortment of polishes and manicure implements.

Beth Ann seemed troubled about something, opening her mouth and closing it several times.

"Out with it! You may never get another chance to lay it on me." Ashley grinned.

Beth Ann shaped a pink nail and held it up for a squint-eyed inspection. "You haven't asked about Dave."

"It didn't seem to be any of my business. I figured if you wanted to bring it up again, you would."

"I do care what you think, and I want you to know that Dave and I parted ways permanently."

Ashley squeezed Beth Ann's arm. "If that's what you want, Beth Ann."

"It is."

"Did you ever get around to talking to Mike?"

She shook her head, sending the feathery curls into motion. "Actually it was his fourteen-year-old daughter, Patti, who brought me up against the truth, although she doesn't realize it."

"Really?"

"Mike asked me to come stay with Patti and young John while he made an emergency hospital call. Patti was doing some homework and practiced a speech she was making to the class. It had to do with the certainty of consequences that follow assault, murder—all the crimes of passion. And do you know she included abortion, venereal disease, and self-destruction? She called them the consequences one pays for crimes of passion committed—against one's own body. Can you believe that from a fourteen-year-old?"

"Marvelous maturity," Ashley agreed. "But what's just as marvelous is that God forgives even those crimes of passion. I worked for a while last year as a volunteer at a clinic for unwed mothers. All of them carried such a sense of guilt. They couldn't forgive themselves, and therefore were unable to receive God's forgiveness. It took a lot of counseling to help them believe that God truly saw them as new creatures and that the stain of immorality was completely obliterated by the blood that stained the cross!"

Beth Ann's short brown curls bobbed in agreement. "Mike says he runs into the same thing. He has considered starting a counseling group for just such a reason. We're going to visit several around the state to get ideas,"

Ashley listened to Beth's excited chatter, most of which included Mike. There was an unmistakable shine in her eyes.

Later in bed Ashley wondered, had Beth Ann found her niche? If so, she certainly hoped it came out better for Beth Ann than it had for her. A patch of light fell on the carpet beneath her window as she slept for the last night under the Florida moon.

Chapter Thirteen

Fall preened itself in rich color in Chicago. Familiar with every crack, crevice and carved initial in the sidewalk, Ashley ambled along toward her house. This was the street where she had hopscotched through childhood, skinned her knees on roller skates, and learned to ride a bike. The flaming maple tree overhead had been a place to hide in summer among leafy branches with a favorite book. In winter it had fascinated her by reaching out spindly fingers to etch a pattern in the sky. In spring, it was a place for robins to return, and now, just like the robin, she had completed her own migration. Red, gold, and orange leaves showered around her golden hair like confetti. With the wind blowing her silver-gray, full-skirted dress into a swirl, she might have been the spirit of autumn.

Her heart was full of pain—the pain of loving—alone. Even if Marc cared, he had not cared enough to save her shop, not enough to relinquish Sydney when to do so would put him at a business disadvantage.

She sighed and kicked aside a rubble of leaves. She had been so sure that Signature Interiors was the right thing for her, but now she understood. God's will was not cast in concrete, but in a pliable substance called surrender. His will was a life process wrought by change, but he remained unchanging.

177

As she neared her parents' rambling white house, she saw her sister-in-law signing for a special delivery letter. Paula and Brad had moved into her parents' home to protect it from vandals during their absence.

It's for you, Ashley," Paula smiled, her brown eyes crinkling at the corners.

Ashley glanced at the return address and saw it was from Perone Enterprises. "Good!" she exclaimed. "It's probably the final payment of my fee." She tore the envelope open eagerly and scanned the contents:

"Reports indicate the Windsong project still has a number of unfinished details. It is company policy to issue payment upon total satisfaction of the contract; therefore, we are requesting your immediate return to complete the job. Enclosed is an airline reservation. Stan will meet your flight at the Tampa airport to fill you in further. Marc."

Tears of humiliation filled Ashley's blue eyes. She headed determinedly for the phone, planning to confront him with the injustice of his demands. The unfinished details were minor and could easily be finished by someone else. She dialed the number and wet her lips nervously. She was afraid he would win the argument. Marc was both persuasive and determined—and she would melt at the very sound of his voice. The number rang once and she dropped the receiver into its cradle. *Coward!* she berated herself.

She sighed, and the beautifully shaped lips drooped sadly. Marc knew where she was vulnerable. She had to have the money to repay Brad's loan. Perhaps if she worked very efficiently, she could still complete the job and get away before Marc returned from Alaska. She would give it her best shot—and this time, she wouldn't leave without the money!

Emerald palms with circlets of topaz chrysanthemums at their base stood around the Tampa International Airport. There was a diamond-like sparkle in the air, and Ashley realized how much she had missed this beauty, even in so short a time.

Stan loaded her bags in the trunk of his Chrysler Imperial and came around to the driver's side. Soon they were out of the city and passing into familiar countryside. He had been strangely silent, not at all like the overbearing belligerent man who had pushed her patience to the limit on several occasions. In fact, he treated her with humble deference that could almost be construed as fear. For several miles he was preoccupied, as though rehearsing what he had to say. At last, the short, stocky figure hitched himself higher in his seat and cleared his throat nervously.

"Ashley, there's something I have to explain to you."

"Yes, Marc said you would," she said dryly. "Apparently there is some dissatisfaction over the completion of Windsong."

"This has nothing to do with Windsong," Stan muttered uncomfortably. "It has to do with Signature Interiors."

Ashley swung her head around in surprise and concentrated on his face as he continued. "Your business location was to have been excluded from the block of buildings sold by Perone Enterprises."

"I don't believe you," she said flatly.

"It's true. However, there were complications in the sale. The bank denied a loan to the purchaser because the appraisal wasn't high enough without the solid block of buildings. The stipulation was that the entire block must be included for the loan to be granted."

Realization dawned in Ashley's mind. "Let me guess. Sydney played her trump card, right? She was the loan officer who set the terms?"

"Right," Stan mumbled apologetically. "To sweeten the pot, she offered to buy the shop and inventory from the new owners at a handsome profit to them, so naturally they put the pressure on me to acquire Signature Interiors."

Ashley's face twisted painfully. "Sydney would stop at nothing to be rid of me. And of course Marc agreed to the terms in order to close the deal."

"Wrong!" Stan declared and produced a letter from the briefcase. "I acted on my own. Marc had already gone to Alaska and was out on one of the pipeline stations where he couldn't be reached. I had to use my own judgment." He sighed heavily. "It was bad judgment."

She scanned the paper Stan had handed her. It was a scathing letter Marc had written to Stan, ordering him to make full explanation to Ashley. He was to procure the deed from Sydney and put it into Ashley's name, free and clear. Failure to do so would result in dismissal from the company.

Ashley was appalled at Marc's stringent action. He was hard. "Sydney would sell it back?"

"She has no choice. Due to her present relationship with Marc, she'll do exactly as he says."

Ashley's heart plummeted. For a moment, there had been hope that Marc cared. No doubt all he cared about was getting her off his conscience. It was Sydney he wanted, and apparently Sydney was willing to sell the shop back to insure that relationship.

They were turning onto the road that led to Windsong, when Ashley got to the business at hand. "I presume you have a list prepared?"

Stan grunted. "Marc will take care of that."

"Marc! He's not here, is he?" Then she saw the Porsche parked in the driveway. "He's supposed to be still be in Alaska. What's he doing here?"

"Waiting for you, I imagine," Stan said soberly, reaching across to open the door.

Ashley stood in front of the old mansion and looked at it through the twilight. How different it looked now. Proud, stately, the fountains sparkling, tinkling, in a twilight song. The pink-stuccoed Spanish design, so popular in central Florida at the turn of the century, had survived as a monument to the past—a past in which citrus was king in an empire of sand hills and crystal lakes. Now it was destined to become the object of curiosity, appreciated only by occasional visitors who would gape at its graces.

The arched windows glowed softly with light, and Ashley knew she could no longer put off the inevitable confrontation with Marc. She strolled to the palm court and paused within its peaceful walls, sure now that this project had been right for her. She was wiser for the experience and more steadfast in the faith that had stood the test.

The soft silk dress whispered as she moved gracefully toward the front door. The fabric was the same shade as her moon-kissed hair. Marc stood with his back to her, looking through the arched windows at the lake. He turned and for a moment stared at her. He offered a perfunctory greeting, but made no move to bridge the barrier of emotions.

Ashley was prepared for anger or reprimand, but not this coolness. He was unapproachable. "I—got your message," she stammered awkwardly.

"So I see. Shall we begin?" he nodded at her briefcase and she quickly removed a note pad and pencil.

"I notice the cornice boards are not installed yet. I'll take care of that immediately." She made a notation. "Also, I see the replacement tiles have arrived. What next?"

Mute, he led the way to the kitchen. Ashley followed his broad shoulders across the room, her heart beating wildly as she went. The camel sweater and matching slacks fit his trim, muscular form superbly, and she longed to be held close to him.

"I've decided to expose the hearth as you suggested originally. You'll need to bring in experts at restoration for this sort of thing. Have an architect draw up several designs for the pit seating around it and submit those to me. This will need to be started immediately, and oh—

be sure the etched words of the wind song are preserved at any cost."

Chagrined, Ashley realized this would take weeks, but said only, "I'm sure the historical society will be pleased."

He raised his eyebrows quizzically, but led the way to the library. All the desks, file cabinets, and the computer had been removed. But, of course, they would be, she realized. Marc had told Nikos he wanted all business terminated by the end of the month. Only the ornate desk and bookshelves remained.

Marc was measuring a space with his hands where he wanted glass display cases for the family archives. Important documents, photographs, and memorabilia would be kept in them. She was pleased that he had remembered her suggestion, but surprised that he intended relinquishing this last link with his past.

Thoughtfully, she said, "Shall I have a brass plate engraved stating these papers are only on loan to the historical society in case you should change your mind and want them back some day?"

The deep furrowed lines across his brow drew into a frown. "What has the historical society got to do with it?" he asked, half amused, half annoyed.

"Everything, I should think. After all, they've acquired the property, haven't they?"

"Decidedly not!" Marc bristled. "Whatever gave you that idea?"

"The executive committee, themselves!" Ashley spurted, more than a little confused. "The afternoon I showed them through the house, they were very excited at having the property. Actually, I thought it was a lovely thing to do since you were liquidating real estate holdings here."

"Wait a minute, hold it!" Marc almost shouted, holding up a restraining hand. "You're going too fast for me. The historical society was told it could open Windsong as a part of the holiday tour of homes the last week in

November. Since I'll not be moving into Windsong until December, I granted them permission to include the mansion on their itinerary." He gave a thoughtful chuckle as he remembered, "In fact, that's why I had to give you a definite deadline. The historical society was fast becoming the hysterical society for fear you wouldn't finish in time."

Ashley's head spun dizzily as she tried to comprehend his words. Easing herself into a chair she squeaked, "Moving in? Moving in! I thought you were moving to Alaska! Your personal office is moved."

"Of course it is! It was only a temporary setup while my staff and I were trying to merge my Alaskan company and Perone Enterprises here. Nikos is an expert in the area of mergers—he knows all the federal regulations. The only way I could keep Perone Enterprises in the citrus industry after all the trouble we've had this year was to merge the assets of both companies."

"And I thought you were giving up."

"I was thinking about it. But then something happened that gave me reason to see that Windsong survived." His voice trailed off and he looked at her broodingly.

Ashley remembered the day at the lakeside and Stan's words. "I'd put my money on Sydney any day. She always gets what she wants—and she wants Windsong." Was she Marc's reason for seeing that Windsong survived? Would Sydney live in the grand old mansion after all?

"Come upstairs," he said. "We have some unfinished business in the master bedroom suite."

He slipped his arm around her as they ascended the staircase. Weak with pleasure at his nearness, she wondered if she would ever be able to subdue her overwhelming love for him.

Marc complimented the lovely appointments in the master suite. He confirmed her wisdom in leaving the gracefully arched, high ceiling with its carved relief border.

"I do see your earlier point about the overwhelming proportions of the room, however. Go ahead and have the privacy drapes made for the posters and canopy on the bed."

She studied him quietly. Why was he doing this? So far, he had gone along with all the changes she had so enthusiastically recommended, almost as though— Yet, she dared not even hope.

"Is there time to order the fabric and have them made for the tour of homes?" he asked.

"If you're sure that's what you want, yes. The new mistress of Windsong might like to state a preference," she suggested. "Have you thought about her?"

"Constantly!" His voice was a throaty whisper. "Night and day." His dark brown eyes held hers suspended. "I think she'll approve the choice. My only concern is whether she'll approve another choice I'll offer her." He spoke with a deep timbre of emotion.

The early evening breeze blew through the open doors of the balcony and quietly folded about the two who stood face to face.

"Oh, Ashley," he breathed huskily, taking her in his arms. "I love you so much." His words were tender, but his touch held her firmly in his grip, willing her to accept him. She reached for his kiss. Its passionate tenderness forever bound her heart. He crushed her against him and she trembled at his embrace. Love spread through her, soothing her crumpled heart.

"I love you, my darling, Marc."

He kissed her again, deeply, completely. Her hands wonderingly caressed his eyes, his mouth, the wonderful strong planes of his face.

"Oh, Marc, I've longed for this moment from the beginning. That is how long I've loved you."

He laughed softly, nuzzling a silky tress away from her ear as he whispered, "Not quite from the beginning, my dear. The night we first met when I rescued you from the storm like a bedraggled little kitten, you thought I was an ogre equal to Blackbeard himself."

"I still do, especially when you take off for Alaska with just the barest good-bye."

"Not guilty! I called you at your shop to tell you we had some serious talking to do when I got back, but you had a customer in the shop—remember, hmmm?"

She grinned. "I wasn't too pleasant as I recall."

"I wanted to shake you and tell you I loved you all at the same time."

Arms locked in embrace, he pulled her down to sit beside him on the chaise lounge.

"I can't believe it's true," she sighed, "me—you."

"And that spells 'us' together, always." He lifted her hand to his lips. "I want you to marry me, Ashley. Will you?"

"I thought you'd never ask."

"I thought I might never get the chance. The way you packed up and left—you might have given me the benefit of the doubt instead of assuming the worst." he snorted.

She shook her head. "I was too hurt, Marc. I thought I knew you, and there's nothing worse than being disappointed by someone you love. Bit by bit, I learned to love the kindness in you; when I learned of your generosity, I loved you for that. I learned to love your growling moments, because even then you were fair. But I learned another thing—that business is your mistress. One thing I haven't learned, Marc. Why did you come back from Alaska two weeks early?"

"Three. Don't you know, really?" He ruffled her hair. "When I heard Stan had used his power of attorney to sell the Signature Interiors location and that you had moved back to Chicago, I went wild. I fired Stan on the spot, and he would still be fired if it weren't for Howis. I was furious with you too. I had been so sure you loved me, and the thought that you might not absolutely struck terror in me. I suddenly knew that nothing I was working for—the merger, Windsong—was worth anything unless I could share it with you."

"Marc, I didn't want to leave. I had no choice. Everything I wanted was gone when the shop was sold. I thought you didn't care for me at all." She lifted tearful eyes to him. "Even then I would have trusted you, but you had never mentioned a lasting commitment. Without that, there was no reason to stay. Do you understand?"

"I do now. I wanted to ask you to marry me the night of the hurricane." He choked as he remembered the danger. "You were so unselfish! I knew for a certainty what my heart had suspected all along—I wanted you for my wife. I wanted your beauty; I wanted your faith; I wanted your honesty; your laughter. But most of all, I wanted your love. I almost proposed to you that night." He released her and strode to the balcony. Gripping the stone balustrade, he stared at the clouds.

Ashley came up beside him. "Why didn't you, Marc?"

Long moments passed before he finally answered. "Because I made the mistake once of planning a marriage before my business affairs were in order. I was bitterly disappointed when Alicia married my brother. I wanted the same kind of trust and faithfulness my ancestor found—a woman who would walk barefoot around the world to be at my side." He turned to her with heartrending honesty. "When I thought I had lost you, too, I saw for the first time how wrong my priorities were. Without you, the rest was ashes."

He wrapped her in his arms and molded her to him. "I may never let you go." He kissed her hungrily.

"I almost came to Chicago after you, but I knew my chances would be better if I could get you back to Windsong. I knew you loved this house, whether or not you did me."

"I love you more, Marc," she said somberly.

He stroked the lovely head that rested on his shoulder. "I know, Ashley. And I can only thank God. I didn't even know for sure that you would come as I requested."

Her laughed rippled. "Demanded is more like it. And yes, you did know that I'd come. You knew I had to have the fee money to pay back Brad's loan."

He grinned mischievously and winked at her. "So I did. All's fair in love and war."

"Speaking of war," Ashley said with snapping eyes. "Stan said Sydney had no choice but to deed Signature Interiors back to me because of her relationship with you. It sounded as if—"

Marc clamped his hand over her mouth. "Shhh. Don't even say it. There has been nothing between us for months, no matter what she may have implied. Stan meant that Sydney is now in my employ—I acquired the bank as part of the merger. One false move and she's out. She used her position for personal gain, and that is strictly forbidden in banking codes. I have it on good authority that she has already begun to transfer Signature Interiors to you."

She made no comment, and Marc said dryly, "I was expecting at least a thank you, and hopefully a whole lot more."

She brushed a feathery kiss on his chin. "I was just thinking, Marc. What if I don't want the shop back?"

"If it's the money you feel you have to return, you know that's no problem. Everything I have is yours."

She sent him a melting glance. "Thank you, Marc, but I wasn't thinking of the money." A softness came into her eyes. "I can never replace Tony and Lita's mother, but I plan to work hard at making my own place in their hearts, and make up for some of their loss. And I want to be the competent keeper of Windsong I know you expect. But most of all, I want to be free of all other responsibilities except for being your wife. Signature Interiors had its time in my life, but it's like a passage to broader and better places." She looked at him sweetly. "Do you mind, darling?"

"Mind?" He kissed her deeply.

The moon had risen high in the sky to make a silvery path across the lake before Ashley removed herself shakily from his arms.

Marc's warm brown eyes strayed to the inviting bedroom chamber, and in a last embrace before he led her downstairs, he whispered, "Let's not wait too long, Ashley."

"We won't," she promised.

On a sunny morning three weeks later, Ashley went to meet her bridegroom under the gazebo that had been transformed into a wedding bower. Beth Ann led the way down the grass-carpeted dock that was festooned with swags of flowers and ferns. Tony bore the ring proudly, and Lita dropped petals, paving the way for Ashley, borne on her father's arm.

Ashley stepped lightly and savored the high moment of her life. As she neared her bridegroom and their glances locked, she suddenly wanted to show him that her life was truly his, under God, and that there was no hardship they could not weather.

A sparkle came to her eyes. Marc, knowing her as he did, waited expectantly. She paused, and in a graceful motion before the astonished guests, she calmly stepped out of one shoe and tossed it into the lake.

Marc smiled as the second shoe splashed in the blue water. The string quartet resumed Lohengrin's wedding march as the barefoot bride stepped demurely to meet her love.

Forever Romances are inspirational romances designed to bring you a joyful, heart-lifting reading experience. If you would like more information about joining our Forever Romance book series, please write to us:

Guideposts Customer Service
39 Seminary Hill Road
Carmel, NY 10512

Forever Romances are chosen by the same staff that prepares *Guideposts*, a monthly magazine filled with true stories of people's adventures in faith. *Guideposts* is not sold on the newsstand. It's available by subscription only. And subscribing is easy. Write to the address above and you can begin reading *Guideposts* soon. When you subscribe, each month you can count on receiving exciting new evidence of God's Presence, His Guidance and His limitless love for all of us.